EXTREMELY
PUZZLED

THE PUZZLED MYSTERY ADVENTURE SERIES: BOOK 3

P.J. Nichols

Paperback ISBN 978-4-910091-08-2
Hardcover ISBN 978-4-910091-10-5
Audiobook ISBN 978-4-910091-09-9

pjnichols.com

Cover design by Thomas Paehler

For my wife,
You are my rock.

CHAPTER 1

Peter was home alone on a chilly Friday evening in early November. His girlfriend of two and a half years, Nicola, had started a new part-time job at a restaurant a few weeks ago, and they always gave her the busy Friday night shift. He wouldn't dare mention it to Nicola, but he really missed hanging out with her on Fridays. For over two years, they had been going to movies almost every Friday afternoon or evening, so this new routine—and Peter hated new routines—was going to take some time to get used to.

The clock on the wall read 7:47, which meant Peter had been pointlessly channel surfing for well over an hour. Most Grade 10 kids would have been watching one of the latest primetime dramas, or maybe a hockey game, but not Peter. He was flipping around trying to catch any *breaking news* stories. Not about celebrities showing up in restaurants or politicians caught going back on their word, but ones about where the most recent natural disaster or severe weather was occurring.

Zoltan was still Earth's weather god and had another twenty-two years until he would be replaced. But despite his best efforts, the weather was wreaking havoc all over the globe. And it wasn't because Zoltan was just sitting around and twiddling his thumbs. It was due to Earth's immense size, and the fact that there were so many things happening simultaneously. How could Zoltan reduce the intensity of an earthquake in Brazil if he was over in Australia trying to provide some rain to drought-stricken areas? The answer, of course, was that he couldn't.

Peter had spent a month or so researching how much damage—in terms of both dollars and human lives—had happened over the past year. The results of his investigation led him to the only plausible resolution: the carnage being caused by the weather could only be controlled if Zoltan had help. To put it simply, Earth needed at least a few more weather gods.

Peter turned off the TV and went up to his room. He had decided two weeks ago *how* he was going to try to get Zoltan some desperately-needed help, but kept putting off *actually doing it*. Peter wished he hadn't been born with procrastination in his DNA. But his mother refused to let Peter use genes as an excuse; she just called it straight-up laziness.

He sat down at his desk and prepared a few sheets of loose-leaf. He needed to draft a letter that was clear, concise, and direct. But he also wanted to make sure it wouldn't come across as being disrespectful in any way.

* * *

About half an hour later, he had completed a draft that he was reasonably satisfied with. Now all he needed to do was type it up and print it. For the majority of kids his age, typing was as easy as riding a bike. Unfortunately, Peter didn't fall into that category; he typed with two fingers and had to look at the keyboard to search for each and every key. Well, he didn't have to search for the *backspace* key, as he used that one far more than the rest.

Dear Lead Weather Gods,

My name is Peter, the teen who helped trap Xavier a few months back. I am writing to you today with an important request: I would like you to seriously consider assigning more weather gods to Earth. In my opinion, Earth needs at least another 6. Zoltan works around the clock, but Earth is huge, and he simply can't do it on his own. I have attached a spreadsheet to this letter which contains statistics of how much damage the weather is causing here. I totaled up the number of deaths linked to severe weather and natural disasters for each continent. And I also calculated the amount of money spent or lost due to those weather events. The numbers are terrifying. There must be something you can do.

Sincerely,

Peter

Peter checked his wristwatch. It was shortly past nine, and he could hear people stirring around downstairs. His parents and sister were obviously home now, but they hadn't come up to check on Peter yet. Either that or they saw his bedroom door was closed and figured he didn't want to be disturbed.

"Oops, I forgot to plug in the light," Peter said to himself. He was referring to the light hidden in the chimney: the one he turned on whenever he needed to contact Zoltan.

He took the extension cord from its hiding place in the closet, plugged it in, and opened his bedroom window. The cord from the light came to just outside his window, so he plugged it into the extension cord and voila, the light came on. Since it was cold outside, he closed the window as much as he could without pinching the cord.

He wanted to leave the light on for at least an hour, so he decided to head back downstairs. Sophia was already in bed, and his parents were sitting at the kitchen table having some chamomile tea.

"Hey, Pete," his dad said. "You want some tea?"

"No, I'm good," Peter replied.

"Are you sure?" his mom asked. "It's a very effective way to help people relax and calm down before bed."

Peter's parents must have thought his visit to the kitchen was because he couldn't fall asleep.

"No, I'm fine, really," he said. "But thanks for the tip. I know where you keep the teabags, so maybe I'll give it a go the next time I find myself tossing and turning at midnight."

Peter went into the living room and continued where he'd left off: flipping through channels to see if any new weather problems were being reported. When Peter's mind got locked onto something, he became obsessed with it. Even if he had wanted to do something else tonight, his brain would never let him.

CHAPTER 2

He woke up way too early the next morning, but this was nothing neither new nor rare for the overly anxious Peter. If he had received a dollar for every minute he had spent awake staring at the ceiling, he would already have enough to buy himself a car.

He knew flopping around in bed was nothing more than a useless waste of time, so he decided to get up and go downstairs to eat. But since Peter's mom turned the furnace down before she went to bed every night, this task was going to be much easier said than done. The chilly air in his room was very uninviting compared to the warmth of his blanket.

He quietly walked downstairs, turned on the kitchen light, and pushed the lever on the thermostat a couple centimeters to the right. Then he let out a yawn and opened up the fridge.

Although Peter was an amazingly creative kid, his breakfasts certainly didn't demonstrate it. He prepared his bowl of cornflakes with milk and a tall glass of orange juice—the same breakfast he had been eating since he was about five. It wasn't that he didn't want to eat something different; he was just worried his stomach might get upset if he did. Basically, he ate the same thing every morning to give him one less thing to worry about.

He knew his mom's razor-sharp ears would hear him moving about at such an early hour, so he chose to use a plastic bowl, spoon, and cup.

Peter took little or no pleasure in his morning breakfast ritual, and he was finished eating in less than six minutes. He left his empty bowl, spoon, and cup on the table—another bad habit he was regularly scolded for—and went back to his bedroom.

With too much on his mind and no way to speed up the clock, Peter started pacing around in circles. He read and reread the note for the lead weather gods so many times that he'd quickly memorized the whole thing without even having tried.

After what felt like an eternity, eight o'clock finally arrived, so Peter got changed, brushed his teeth, and got ready to go. He needed to tell a *little white lie* about where he was going, as he certainly couldn't tell his mom and dad he was off to meet up with a weather god! So he started writing a note saying that he and Neil were going to the mall. But just as he was finishing the note, his mom came into the kitchen to turn on the coffee maker.

"*You* are going to the mall?" his mom asked. "But you hate the mall."

"Well, Neil needs help choosing a Christmas present for Claire," Peter replied, digging himself deeper into his lie. "And I couldn't say no."

"Yo, Pete," Bradley yelled from the family room. Peter was a little startled, as he didn't know Bradley was already up. "I'm heading there, too. Well, not this instant, but pretty soon. Wanna lift?"

"Nah," Peter answered nervously. "I'll ride there. I need the exercise."

"You sound like Dad, man," Bradley laughed. "Don't tell me you're gonna start counting calories, too?"

"I heard that!" Peter's dad said loudly while walking down the stairs.

"Anyway," Peter said before Bradley had a chance to reply. "It's fine. I'll ride. That way Neil and I can come home whenever we want."

"Suit yourself," Bradley replied. "But you can't say I didn't offer."

Peter went back upstairs and put on a few layers of clothes to get ready for his chilly ride. Luckily snow hadn't fallen yet this year, but it was bound to one day very soon.

* * *

Peter arrived at Silverhead Mountain shortly after nine o'clock. It was a rarity for Peter to ever be late, but today he had to stop a couple times to take off layers when he got too sweaty. He ended up arriving three minutes and fifteen seconds past the designated time.

Zoltan was sitting at one of the picnic tables and turned to wave to Peter as he rode up.

Peter was shocked at the drastic change in Zoltan's appearance since the last time they had met, which was only about five weeks ago. Zoltan looked like he had aged a few years, or perhaps hadn't slept a wink in days.

"Zoltan," Peter said in a tone that clearly conveyed how worried he was. "Are you okay? Are you sick or something?"

"No," he replied. "But thanks for asking. I'm just burnt out. Totally burnt out. Earth's weather is a nightmare to control. Well, I guess I technically should've known that all along, but I never took my responsibilities seriously until a few months ago." Zoltan paused. "But I didn't come here to complain. I came because you asked me to. So, what's up?"

Although Peter was slowly improving his communication skills, he always found it difficult to choose the right words to start with. "I, uh," he said, "uh, I wrote a letter."

"A letter?" Zoltan asked.

"Yeah," Peter replied, suddenly feeling anxious

for no reason at all. "It's for the lead weather gods."

"You wrote those guys a letter?" Zoltan asked, looking very surprised.

"Well," Peter said. "You are welcome to read it first if you want. It's a request that they send more weather gods here to help you out. You know, like, maybe half a dozen or so."

"Half a dozen?" Zoltan said with a smile. "Peter, I have been requesting backup for over two months. And every time I make a request, I always get the same reply: *We don't have anyone available to spare.*"

"But don't they know how many people are dying because Earth is too big to manage on your own?" Peter asked.

"They do," he replied. "And they sincerely care. The fact of the matter is that there are no fully-trained weather gods available who aren't already assigned somewhere else."

"What do you mean," Peter asked, "by fully-trained?"

"To become a weather god," Zoltan began, "you have to attend a special school for your education, training, and practice. I suppose one could compare it to what you call a *university* here on Earth. But from start to finish, it takes ten years to complete."

"Ten years?!" Peter reacted in disbelief. "Why so long?"

"There's a lot more to controlling the weather than meets the eye," Zoltan answered with a wink. "The techniques we use are extremely difficult to master. Over eighty percent of the students who enter the school drop out because it's too hard. And if you don't graduate, then you are not qualified to be a weather god."

"But still," Peter said with a befuddled look on his face, "there are plenty of graduates every year, right? So why can't they just send a bunch of them here to help?"

"Unfortunately, it doesn't work that way," Zoltan replied while shaking his head. "Things are pretty archaic as far as the system goes. All planet assignments are done once every fifty years, which means everyone switches planets on the exact same day. And right now we are twenty-eight years into the current cycle."

"So what do all the new graduates do?" Peter asked. "Don't tell me they just sit around and wait for the next fifty-year cycle to start. That's ridiculous!"

"You're completely right," Zoltan agreed. "It is ridiculous. But that's just how they do it."

"What do all the graduates do while they wait all those years?" Peter asked, feeling more agitated by the minute.

"Various things," Zoltan explained. "Some take on part-time teaching positions at the school. Some do at-home tutoring for students. A few have even opened up a prep school: you know, to help kids who want to enter the training school get the skills they need to pass the entrance exam. And there are others who decide to get into the research side of things. Instead of becoming weather gods, they try to discover new and more effective ways of controlling the weather."

There was a long and uncomfortable pause in the conversation. Peter wanted to ask something, but he knew it would just sound like another complaint about their bizarre system.

"However," Zoltan said, breaking the silence, "I will take your letter and spreadsheets back to planet Sevlar, which some people refer to as the planet of the weather gods, and deliver them in person. I'm not sure it will initiate any sort of drastic change, but it certainly can't hurt. After all, you are extremely respected on Sevlar, as it was *your* ingenious plan that led to the capture of Xavier."

"Really?" Peter said with a bit of a grin. "You mean, they actually talk about me there?"

"They do more than just talk about you," Zoltan answered. "The history textbook used for twelve-year-olds is currently being rewritten to include a new chapter, dedicated specifically to explaining what you did and how important it was."

"You mean," Peter said, feeling proud and embarrassed at the same time, "kids on Sevlar will be taught about me?"

"You've already become a household name," Zoltan replied while holding up his hand for a high-five. "And after the textbook gets republished, the younger generation will know everything about you."

"Cool!" Peter said, high-fiving Zoltan's hand hard.

"I promise I'll deliver what you've just given me to the lead weather gods today," Zoltan said. "And return tomorrow to tell you how it went. Meet me back here at ten o'clock again."

"How do you get there and back so fast?" Peter asked.

"Let's save that explanation for another day," Zoltan replied.

"Okay," Peter said. "Anyway, good luck. I'll keep my fingers crossed."

"Keep your fingers crossed?" Zoltan asked, awkwardly trying to cross his fingers on both hands. "Why would you do that? How would you write? Or how would you ride your bike? Or—"

"Let's save that explanation for another day," Peter said with a big grin. "Off you go."

CHAPTER 3

Peter ended up having a power nap on the sofa mid-afternoon, which helped him feel somewhat refreshed. He found it amazing how thirty minutes of sleep on the sofa seemed to make up for three or four hours of missed sleep the previous night. He was really looking forward to tonight, as he and Nicola were going out for an early dinner, followed by a movie. Nicola had miraculously managed to convince her boss to give her the lunch shift today, so she was off at three o'clock. She had told Peter that she needed time to shower after work, plus she wanted to take a quick nap before heading out, so they had set five o'clock as the meet-up time.

One of the most awkward things about "date night" for two young people without driver's licenses was the transportation issue. You either had to get dropped off and picked up by a nosey parent or older sibling, or you had to take the bus. Unfortunately, bus service in Clearville was abysmal. The closest bus stop to Peter's home was a twelve-minute walk, and there was only one bus an hour on weekends.

The last time they'd gone out, Nicola's mom had been their "chauffeur," so today it was Peter's turn to sort out how they'd get to the movie. He couldn't ask his older brother Bradley, as he was away for the entire weekend at a big indoor track and field competition. So that left his mom and dad as his only two options, both of which had their pros and cons.

His mom was the "queen of punctuality," so she would definitely get them to where they wanted to go, and back, at exactly the times requested. But along with her punctuality came her fairly irritating habit of dominating the conversation for the full journey both ways.

His dad was also reliable as far as time was concerned, but having him as the driver included the risk that he'd fire off an array of outrageous questions to Nicola. Peter's dad had unintentionally embarrassed him more times than he cared to recall.

* * *

When Peter and Nicola were still a fairly new couple back in Grade 8, his dad had happily agreed to drop them off, and then later pick them up, from a concert they had tickets to in the neighboring city of Stoneburg. The drive there was thankfully free of any ridiculous comments, but the ride back was another story. When they hopped in the car after what had been an awesome concert, instead of asking how the concert was—the most natural thing anyone would ask—Peter's dad turned around and directly asked Nicola, "If I offered you fifty dollars to cut off your long hair, would you do it?"

She was so stunned by the obscurity of the question that she had to ask for clarification. "My hair? For fifty bucks? Why?" she asked back.

"Don't answer a question with a question," his dad said in what almost sounded like a condescending tone. "Fifty bucks. Yes or no?"

* * *

The thing Peter seemed to have forgotten today was that he may not be able to choose who to ask. Just because his parents were in their late forties didn't necessarily mean that they both always stayed home all weekend.

He went to the backyard where they were both busy raking up the autumn leaves. Their house was a bit old, but it came with a huge yard and garden. When the leaves changed colors in fall, the backyard was absolutely stunning.

"Pete, come here," his dad said. "I want to show you something."

Peter knew that whenever his dad *wanted to show him something*, that it meant whatever was about to occur would involve little "showing." Peter was ninety-nine percent sure that his dad was about to hand him the rake and then go inside to catch the end of a golf tournament on TV.

"Stephen, don't make Peter do your work," his mom said sternly. "You know he's got a date with Nicola tonight. He probably came out to ask if one of us can drive them."

Peter hadn't mentioned anything about tonight's date to either of his parents, or Bradley, or even his younger sister Sophia. "How do you know Nik and I are going out tonight?" he asked with curiosity.

"I heard you talking on the phone with her last night," his mom answered. "If you want your conversations to be private, you'll need to speak a LOT more quietly."

Peter had indeed spoken to Nicola on the phone the previous night, but had done so in his room with the door shut. Either his mom has superhuman hearing, or the thin wall separating his bedroom from theirs lacked sufficient sound insulation.

"Your father will be happy to drive you," she said without even conferring with Stephen first. "Right?"

Peter's dad knew the consequences of putting up even the slightest resistance in this type of situation, so he immediately nodded and then responded, "No sweat." But Peter knew his dad didn't really mind. He'd probably stop by the driving range and hit a couple hundred balls after dropping them off.

CHAPTER 4

Nicola's house wasn't even a five-minute drive from their place, which meant leaving by 4:55 would get them there on time. But for some strange reason, Peter's dad kept hassling him to hurry up and get ready.

"Dad," Peter explained. "There's no point in leaving so early. We'll just end up sitting in her driveway waiting."

"And by the way," his dad responded, tossing the keys to Peter unexpectedly. "*You* are driving us there. You're old enough to drive as long as I am in the car with you, right?"

Peter had obtained his learner's permit shortly after turning fourteen, so he was technically allowed to drive as long as he was with an adult. He was actually signed up for driving lessons this coming January, so there was no reason for his dad to put him behind the wheel today.

But before Peter had a chance to plead his case, his dad was already sitting in the passenger seat, seatbelt done up snugly.

"Dad, you know I've never driven anywhere other than an empty parking lot," Peter mentioned. "And I've only done that twice."

"Life in the fast lane," Peter's dad replied, an answer which made absolutely no sense. But Peter was long since used to the way his dad used proverbs and other sayings completely out of context.

"You're only driving until we get to Nicola's place," his dad answered. "And the streets to get there are all residential. You won't see another moving car, I promise."

"But we still don't have to leave yet," Peter said. "We can—"

"Things to do, people to see, places to go," his dad said, interrupting him.

Peter realized, like it or not, that he was going to have to start driving immediately. He slowly backed out of the driveway and started to head toward Nicola's home.

"Turn left here," his dad said suddenly.

"But Nik's house is straight, not—"

"Just turn left," his dad repeated. "There's something you have got to see."

"Oh, here we go again," Peter whispered to himself so that his dad wouldn't hear him over the radio. He knew he was about to be led "somewhere" to see "something" he'd have no interest in.

"Now go right," his dad instructed. "And park up at the end of that cul-de-sac."

Peter did as he was told, and the second he put the car into park, his dad opened the door and hopped out. "Come on, we don't have much time," his dad said as he shut the door.

Peter reluctantly got out, carefully checked that he'd locked the doors—something completely unnecessary considering where they were—and jogged to catch up to his dad. He followed him through the walkway between two of the houses at the end of the cul-de-sac.

"Check it out," his dad proudly announced, pointing at the big, yellow piece of construction equipment in front of them. "They brought in that excavator last Sunday, but it hasn't done any work yet. I wonder what they are going to do or build here?" He paused as if waiting for Peter to enthusiastically jump into the conversation. All Peter did was look at his watch.

"Dad, we gotta head back to the car," Peter said, tossing the keys to his dad. "If we don't go soon, we'll end up being late getting to Nik's. And you know how much I hate being late."

* * *

Peter and Nicola decided to try something different for a change, so they went to a new Greek restaurant that had just opened in October. It was within walking distance of the movie theater, so it seemed like a logical choice—and

Peter, above all things, always chose logical.

The food was great, the waiter was funny, and the atmosphere of the restaurant was perfect. But despite all of those positives, it was clear to Nicola that a big chunk of Peter's mind was somewhere else.

"Okay, Pete," she said right after they ordered dessert. "I'll be blunt. You've barely said anything tonight, other than meaningless one-word comments about the food. And even those sounded more or less robotic. Don't get me wrong here. I'm not trying to tell you I'm bored. I'm just, well, confused."

Peter felt his throat tighten. He knew he'd been acting a little odd, but it certainly wasn't intentional. He was just preoccupied with the upcoming meeting with Zoltan. And he figured blabbering on about that meeting would be selfish and rude, which could potentially ruin the evening.

"Pete," she said, taking his hand. "I'm your girlfriend. I'm not going to get angry or anything like that. Just tell me what's going on inside that busy mind of yours."

With the open invitation to speak freely, Peter rapidly went through everything that had happened earlier that day. Nicola remained silent as she listened intently, nodding every so often to indicate that she was following along.

As soon as he finished, she playfully punched

him in the shoulder and said, "That's what's been eating at you? Oh, man... I thought you were going to tell me something serious like you were thinking of breaking up."

Peter got goose bumps from just hearing that phrase. Nicola was the perfect girlfriend.

"Break up with you?" he said timidly. "I'd never do that. You're, like, too perfect."

Nicola stood up from her seat and walked to the other side of the table. She leaned down and hugged Peter from behind.

"Aw, aren't you just the sweetest," she whispered in his ear. "You're pretty perfect yourself, too. But PLEASE be more honest the next time something is bugging you. I don't want to have to drag it out of you like I did today."

"I promise, I promise," he answered quickly, feeling embarrassed that quite a few people sitting nearby were now looking their way.

"And if you think I'm going to end this hug just because you're embarrassed everyone is looking at us," Nicola continued, obviously reading Peter's mind, "then you are wrong with a capital *W.* You'll just sit there and let me hug you for as long as I want."

* * *

Since they both knew Peter wouldn't be capable of focusing on a movie tonight, they decided to go to a coffee shop near the theater instead. They chose a table in the far corner so they could talk about the whole Zoltan situation without being overheard.

Nicola agreed that Peter's letter was a good idea, but figured it would probably amount to nothing. And she also informed him that she was coming along to meet Zoltan tomorrow.

"But don't you have to do a history paper that's due on, like, Tuesday?" Peter asked.

"Of course I do," she replied, drinking the last of her cafe latte. "But I'm sure my *too perfect* boyfriend would be happy to come to the library to help out with the research after we finish talking with Zoltan, wouldn't he?"

CHAPTER 5

Rain hammered down on Peter's bedroom window that night. It, along with the gusting wind, seemed unrelenting. His room overlooked their big backyard, and the branches of the huge trees were blowing so hard that Peter figured it was only a matter of time before one would snap off and come smashing through his window.

It sounded like the storm just kept growing in power. That being said, Peter was so overly focused on each and every sound it was making that he couldn't be a reliable judge. He really needed to get his mind off the storm, or else he'd drive himself crazy. He tiptoed downstairs, poured himself a glass of milk, and then walked back toward his room.

When he opened his bedroom door, he immediately felt the powerful wind blowing in through the broken window. He spotted the branch on his bed, the one that was obviously responsible for smashing the window. There was also lots of shattered glass both on and around his bed.

One side of Peter's bed was right against the wall with the window in it, so he didn't dare get up on his bed to try to *do something* about the window. Instead, he just stood there, like a statue. After a minute of doing nothing, he decided it was time to go get his parents. But when he spun around to walk out, he stepped on a piece of broken glass, which pierced the soft skin in the arch of his foot. He sat down and looked at the glass shard wedged in his foot and the blood that was dripping out. It hurt, but not nearly as much as it should have. Maybe the psychology professor who had given a guest lecture at their school last month was not joking about the "mind over matter" concept.

* * *

Peter jolted himself awake. That whole crazy storm, broken glass, bleeding foot thing had been nothing more than another one of his wonky dreams.

He was drenched in sweat. Even though it was a dream, his sympathetic nervous system had been fooled into thinking it was completely real. And it wasn't just his clothes that were wet, his sheets and pillowcase were damp as well. Peter technically suffered from a condition his doctor called hyperhidrosis, which in laymen's terms means excessive sweating. But since there was no medicine for this condition, he had to, well, just sweat... a lot...

His heart still racing from the nightmare, Peter peeled off his drenched pajamas and put on a dry pair. Then he threw an extra blanket from his closet on top of the wet sheets, as he was too lazy to bother changing them. Plus he flipped his pillow over to rest his head on the dry side. And then he did the same thing he always did after every one of his silly nightmares: stared at the ceiling, trying to see if he could get the stucco to form any shapes he hadn't spotted previously. He did this, of course, because he knew he wouldn't be getting back to sleep.

CHAPTER 6

Considering the time of year, and the fact it had been so cold yesterday, today was refreshingly warm. This was great news for Peter and Nicola, as they wouldn't have to freeze their butts off riding out to meet Zoltan.

They were in pretty good spirits as they rode to Silverhead Mountain. Although Peter was far too shy to admit it, having Nicola with him today actually meant a lot to him.

* * *

When they turned the corner to head to the picnic tables, what they saw was both fantastic and shocking... Zoltan was not alone! Three other people, whom Peter immediately guessed were weather gods, were sitting at one of the picnic tables.

"Pete! Nicola!" Zoltan said loudly, with a big, welcoming smile. He grabbed Peter's hand and shook it fast and hard, and then gave Nicola a big hug.

But something didn't seem right. Zoltan was acting weird. Or maybe he was just excited?

"Guys," Zoltan continued, "you ARE NOT going to believe this! After I delivered Peter's letter, the lead weather gods called an emergency meeting. Meetings like that are almost NEVER called. Then twenty minutes later, they called me in to see them."

"Twenty minutes? Wow, that was fast," Peter replied. "And I am assuming these three people are the results of that meeting?"

"You got it," Zoltan answered proudly. "Pete and Nicola, everyone on my planet owes you two, Neil, and Bradley a huge debt of gratitude. The ten lead weather gods voted unanimously to send some students to help."

"What do you mean by... help?" Nicola asked.

"Yeah," Peter followed. "You told me yesterday that they never break with tradition. You said they were not permitted to use their abilities outside of school until they'd graduated."

"They made an exception," Zoltan replied, "for the first time in history. These three are all set to graduate in six months' time. And they are the top three in their class. Guys, they sent me the three *best!* Isn't this fantastic?"

"Uh... yeah," Peter said softly, fumbling to find a suitable way to react.

"It's awesome!" Nicola said loudly and clearly, bailing out her tongue-tied boyfriend.

"Come on guys," Zoltan said while starting to head to the picnic table. "I can't wait to introduce you to them."

They followed Zoltan over to the picnic table to meet these three young—and apparently very talented—assistants.

Zoltan was almost uncontrollably excited to do the introductions. As they got closer, it became clear that the group consisted of one man and two women. When they were within a couple of meters, the two women politely stood up, but the man remained seated and didn't even glance their way.

"Allow me to introduce," Zoltan said proudly, "going clockwise: Cynthia, Aurora, and Maximilian. Everyone, this is Peter and Nicola, who you of course already know a lot about."

Peter and Nicola shook hands with Aurora and Cynthia. Maximilian remained seated and completely ignored them.

"Now, come on Maximilian," Zoltan said, hoping that calling him out would encourage him to talk. "Don't be so rude. The least you could do is say hello to these two wonderful teenagers. You know how much we owe them for—"

"Fine," Maximilian blurted out. "Peter, hello. Nicola, hello," he said coldly. Then he turned and stared at Zoltan. "There, satisfied?"

You didn't need to have a degree in psychology or communication to figure out how awkward this was going to be.

"Don't worry about Maximilian," Zoltan laughed, trying to artificially lighten the mood. "He's just tired from the long trip here."

"Peter!" Cynthia jumped in before Maximilian had a chance to debate or argue that point. "My niece and nephew absolutely adore you. They are soooo jealous that I get to meet you in person."

"No way," Peter said, face reddening. "You're exaggerating."

"Not at all," Cynthia replied, pulling out two sheets of fancy-looking paper and a special pen. "I promised them I'd get your autograph if I had the chance."

Peter's face grew even redder.

"Oh, so now you're Mr. Popularity?" Nicola joked, nudging him with her elbow. "Suppose you'll have to start up a fan club and charge a membership fee to join, eh?"

Peter and Zoltan got a good laugh out of that, but obviously "fan clubs" didn't exist on planet Sevlar, as all three students looked confused.

Peter politely accepted the papers and pen, and placed them safely in a folder in his backpack. "I'll sign them later," he said. "After I have a chance to think about what to write."

"Great!" Cynthia replied. "I wrote their names in pencil on the back, as I figured you'd never be able to get the spelling right."

Aurora had been watching the whole exchange

but was politely waiting for her turn, as she didn't want to interrupt. "Peter," she said, "I actually only told my parents about being sent here. If I had told everyone where I grew up, I would have needed a few suitcases to carry all the things they'd have wanted you to sign."

"You're going to need a security team if you ever go to Sevlar," Nicola laughed, almost in stitches from imagining Peter being a rock star or idol.

"Zoltan," Maximilian barked rudely. "We were sent here to help you manage Earth's weather, not to make pointless chit-chat with a bunch of kids. Hurry up and assign me to a continent. I want to get started."

"Settle down, Maximilian," Zoltan replied, with a bit of irritation showing in his voice. Then he turned to Peter and Nicola. "Although Aurora and Cynthia are extremely pleased to spend their final six months of school here, Maximilian DID NOT want to come."

"Yeah," Cynthia added. "You see, Maximilian comes from a family of *very powerful* weather gods, many whom have gone on to become lead weather gods. He thinks he's too good for this."

"I *am* too good for this," Maximilian said loudly, crossing his arms and staring right at Cynthia.

"Look, we know you're way more skillful than Cynthia and me," Aurora said, hoping to reverse the downward spiral of the conversation. "That's why we are so lucky to have you here with us."

"Good on you," Peter whispered to himself. "He certainly can't refute that comment."

"Whatever," Maximilian replied. "But Zoltan, can you please explain why I have to waste my time talking to these kids when I could be practicing?"

"Maximilian!" Cynthia yelled right in his face. "Show Peter and Nicola some respect!"

"It's fine, it's fine," Peter said nervously.

"No, it's NOT fine," Zoltan said. "Maximilian, if you insist on knowing, there are two reasons I am introducing you to these *young adults:* First of all, Peter has a huge amount of data and statistics about where the worst of the weather damage is occurring. Discussing these things will help us in our efforts to get the weather under control. And secondly, and this is more for Aurora and Cynthia since you seem set on being antisocial, Peter here is one of the best puzzle-makers alive. And you know how much everyone on Sevlar loves puzzles and riddles. He and Nicola said they would be happy to come up with a couple of riddles a month to give you some entertainment while you are here."

Before Maximilian had a chance to open his mouth and inject something negative, Zoltan kept talking. "Peter and Nicola," he said. "Please take a seat with my three trainees. There is so much they need to hear from you. Spare no details.

They need to know everything. Give them all the info you can about the current state of things here on Earth."

"Um... okay," Peter replied timidly. "But I don't really know where to start."

"Let's go one continent at a time," Nicola suggested.

"Sure," Peter agreed. "Which one first?"

"Europe," Maximilian said loudly and coldly. "That's where I'm going. And I could care less whether or not the rest of you approve."

* * *

After spending a good forty-five minutes running through the details of Europe, South America, and Africa, Zoltan decided it was time to call it a day. All three trainees were visibly tired, and there was no way they would be able to stay focused enough to take in everything they needed to know about the remaining continents. On top of that, Zoltan couldn't expect Peter and Nicola to spend their entire day here. He instructed his trainees to take a short walk along the river, and be back at the picnic table in twenty minutes.

"Peter, Nicola," Zoltan said once Maximilian, Aurora and Cynthia were out of sight. "Thanks a million."

"No problem," Peter replied.

"And before you head home, I have a big favor to ask," Zoltan continued. "I'm really, really hoping you can come up with a puzzle for them to do next Sunday. You know, it would give them something to look forward to."

"Sure," Peter replied happily.

"And it might even get Maximilian to stop being such a selfish jerk," Nicola said.

"I doubt it," Zoltan laughed, "but it just may help a little."

* * *

Shortly after arriving home, Peter talked to Bradley, phoned Neil, and asked Neil to call Claire. Everyone agreed to try to help come up with an idea to use for the challenge. They all promised to call Peter when they thought of something suitable. Although the obsessive part of Peter's mind wanted to start brainstorming ideas right away, he needed to put that aside for the rest of the afternoon. He had promised Nicola he would join her at the library and help her with research for her history report. Besides, seeing as he had destroyed their date last night, he wanted to "give it his all" this afternoon.

CHAPTER 7

Peter didn't even have to wait twenty-four hours before someone on his "team" came up with a great idea. He was eating lunch with Nicola at school on Monday when Claire and Neil came over and sat down with them. Claire told them her idea, making sure to speak quietly so the group near them wouldn't overhear and wonder what they were talking about. Peter immediately gave her the thumbs up. Not only was it an awesome idea, but it also involved very little preparation. Now that the pressure of thinking up a puzzle was off, Peter felt like he was going to be able to enjoy the rest of the week a lot more.

* * *

All five of them—Peter, Nicola, Neil, Claire, and Bradley—wanted to be there on Sunday morning. Neil, Claire, and Bradley were especially excited, as it was their first time to meet the three trainees. Bradley kindly offered to drive everyone. His car could comfortably fit five, which meant no one would have to cycle there in what was forecast to be a very cold Sunday.

Bradley was a very slow and cautious driver these days. Actually, he had changed his somewhat reckless driving habits a few years back, right after causing an accident. The accident was one hundred percent his fault, but thankfully didn't cause any injuries to anyone in either car.

* * *

The accident had happened when he was seventeen, less than two weeks after he had finally saved up enough money to buy himself an old clunker. As most high school boys do, he and a buddy were cruising around town, tunes cranked, trying to impress any girls their age that happened to be walking beside the road. What they didn't realize back then—and most likely still don't understand now—is that this type of behavior repels more girls than it attracts. (But anyway, that's beside the point...)

Bradley and his friend Thomas had been driving back and forth on the town's main drag for over an hour in the early afternoon. On their sixth or seventh pass of the swimming pool, they spotted two Grade 12 girls walking to the outdoor pool. Of course, heading to the pool meant they were wearing their bikinis and flip flops, which gave Bradley and Thomas something to really focus on. Unfortunately, this *focusing* lasted a few seconds too long, and when Bradley's eyes finally went back to the road, there was a car stopped right in front of him, waiting to make a left turn into the parking lot.

He slammed on the brakes as hard as he could, but there wasn't enough distance between him and the other car. His tires locked, and there was a second or two of rubber screeching on asphalt before the *bang* when his car hit the stationary car.

Luckily for everyone involved, both Bradley and Thomas, and the woman driving the other car, all had had their seat belts on. And the impact had not been all that hard. The two boys quickly hopped out of their car and went to see if the woman, who had no passengers with her, was okay. She said it had scared the living daylights out of her, but that she wasn't hurt in any way.

Then she also got out so they could all survey the damage to the cars. Bradley's front fender looked as if nothing had happened, but the woman's rear bumper and license plate had been dented. As is customary after any car accident, they exchanged insurance and license information. In addition, an eyewitness came up and gave them his name and phone number.

The increase in insurance fees was more than enough to convince Bradley to smarten up when it came to paying attention while behind the wheel. His "fender bender" was going to cost him a total of about two thousand dollars in extra insurance fees over the next three years.

* * *

Just as they had expected, Aurora and Cynthia were eagerly awaiting their arrival, but Maximilian was being completely anti-social again. The two women stood up and started walking over to meet the new arrivals.

"So how'd the first week go?" Peter asked as he got out of Bradley's car. "Must have been a real eye-opener, eh?"

Aurora and Cynthia looked at each other and shrugged their shoulders. Bradley quickly picked up on their body language as an indicator that Peter's choice of words had not been ideal.

"What my little brother was trying to ask," Bradley said, "was if you were surprised by the huge number of weather disasters that are happening all over this planet?"

"It's crazy here on Earth," Aurora answered. "I can't believe they've always just assigned a single weather god here. There should be at least five or six, or maybe even a dozen."

Even though her reply was nothing more than just a simple, honest, and clear one, Bradley hadn't been listening to a single word of it. This had occurred because, in classic Bradley style, he had noticed how incredibly beautiful Aurora was.

Nicola immediately noticed Bradley's expression, which clearly showed he was thinking *wow, this chick is hot!* She couldn't resist the chance to embarrass him a bit. Plus this gave her a fun way to start the official introductions.

"I apologize for Brad's staring, and for Peter's absentmindedness," she said. "Allow me to introduce everyone. Brad, Neil, Claire: meet Aurora, Cynthia, and Maximilian."

Aurora and Cynthia shook hands with Bradley, Neil, and Claire. Bradley's handshake with Aurora appeared to last far longer than was necessary.

When they walked over to Maximilian—whom they'd been warned about in advance—he stuck up his palm and coldly said, "I'm not going to pretend to be friendly and chatty with everyone. I now know your names, and you know mine."

Feeling like he was the unofficial coordinator of today's little event, Zoltan jumped in to get things moving. "These five talented friends of mine have done exactly what I promised they would," he said. "They made a challenge for you to try today."

"An easy one?" Cynthia asked, clearly excited to get started.

"No way," Aurora said to her, "I bet it's super hard. You've heard all the stories about how clever this group is."

"Actually, I know nothing about its difficulty level," Zoltan replied honestly, putting his hands into his pockets and taking a few steps back. "I have absolutely no idea what today's challenge is."

"Don't expect me to take part in this!" Maximilian announced from his seat.

Zoltan elected to pretend he hadn't heard that. But his slightly furrowed brow indicated the stress that Maximilian was causing him.

"The floor is yours," Zoltan said to Peter.

"Not this time," Peter replied. "It's Claire's. She's the one who came up with today's challenge."

Claire was carrying a shoebox with a small envelope taped to the lid. She walked over to the picnic table that Maximilian was sitting at and placed it down very hard right in front of him. It was a no-brainer that she was doing this to make Maximilian understand that, like it or not, he *would* be participating. Her tenure as the volleyball team captain in junior high school had given her enough confidence to challenge people with bad attitudes without worrying about the possible consequences.

"Your instructions are on the note in the envelope," she explained. "And everything you need is in the box. You have one hour to complete this challenge, starting now."

Peter pressed the start button on his wristwatch.

CHAPTER 8

Despite having the shoebox placed right in front of him, Maximilian was acting as if it didn't even exist. Aurora and Cynthia, on the other hand, darted over to the picnic table to see what creative and innovative puzzle lay in store for them.

"Aurora," Cynthia said to her, "why don't you read the note, and I'll check out what's inside the box?"

Aurora quickly pulled the note from the envelope and read it aloud.

> *First of all, we'd like to take this opportunity to welcome you to Earth. We were so glad when we found out that Zoltan had finally been given some talented people to help him!*
>
> *Inside the box, you'll find one golf ball (don't worry, you do not need to know*

what golf is to do this challenge), and a whole bunch of feathers. The feathers were collected yesterday afternoon from the farm of a close friend.

Your task is as follows: You must hold the golf ball and a feather (or a few feathers) at waist level, and let go of both at exactly the same time. The feather(s) must hit the ground before the golf ball does.

The rules: You may bend, twist, contort or combine the feathers in any way you wish, but you may not attach anything to them. Additionally, you are not allowed to wet the feathers. And finally, you can't use things like glue or tape to stick them together.

And that's all! Let's call it the "changing the law of gravity" challenge. Ha, aren't we funny?

Good Luck!

"Can't be done," Maximilian said immediately, despite the fact he had announced just moments ago that he would only be watching.

"Come on, Maximilian," Cynthia said. "You

remember what Zoltan told us, right? How these kids can both solve and make really, really challenging riddles?"

"Yeah," Aurora added. "She wouldn't give us one if it were impossible to solve. That's not how this game works."

Maximilian elected to keep his mouth shut. Even though he had said that he didn't want to take part in this game, something instinctive inside him was compelling him to participate. Just like everyone else from planet Sevlar, he couldn't turn down a challenging riddle.

Aurora picked up the golf ball and one of the feathers. "We all know gravity is gravity," she said. "But the air here may be very different from the air on Sevlar."

She held both at waist level and let go of them simultaneously. The feather started fluttering down very slowly and the golf ball dropped like a rock. (Well, a golf ball pretty much is a rock, isn't it?)

"Eeeps!" she said as the golf ball landed on her toe.

"Eeeps?" Bradley asked, since he was still close enough to hear what they were saying. He was supposed to be sitting with Peter and the rest of the group at a picnic table far away from Maximilian, Aurora, and Cynthia, but had stuck around to get a chance to ogle Aurora a little longer.

She looked at Bradley and smiled, "You mean you don't say *eeps* when you hurt yourself?"

"Nah," Bradley replied, doing his best to look as cool as he could. "We usually say *ouch*."

"Do you realize your senseless exchange with that boy is doing nothing but wasting part of our precious sixty minutes?" Maximilian asked coldly. It looked like he was going to get involved with this puzzle after all.

"Brad, stop flirting!" Nicola yelled from the picnic table they were at. "Or at least hold off until their hour is up!"

Bradley came over and joined them at the picnic table, desperately hoping that Aurora wasn't familiar with the word "flirting."

"Nice one, Nik," Peter said, giving her a high-five. For once, Bradley was the one with the red face.

"Well, why don't we start by examining the feathers more closely?" Cynthia suggested.

"For what?" Maximilian asked, but a little more rudely than he should have.

"I can't answer that," Cynthia replied harshly, looking Maximilian right in the eyes. "But I'd love to hear YOU tell me what to examine."

His cockiness seemed to temporarily vanish, and he stood up to look more closely at the feathers. "Hmm..." he said quite softly. "I wonder how we can significantly reduce the wind resistance?"

"Wind what?" Aurora asked.

"Oh, give me a break, please," Maximilian said, his rude attitude front and center again. "We are talking rudimentary science here."

"Don't speak like that to her!" Cynthia yelled, slamming both hands hard on the picnic table. "Even though you may be a big *know-it-all,* it does not give you the right to talk rudely to others."

Although Maximilian didn't apologize, he did seem to show a shift in attitude after that comment. "The reason a feather falls so slowly," he explained, "is due to, uh... resistance. Air resistance. Which means, uh... basically that, uh..."

"Well, at least you're trying," Cynthia commented. "Allow me to help. Aurora, air looks clear, right? But it's actually composed of countless tiny particles. A feather can't push through those as easily as a golf ball can. Feathers are supposed to be like that. That's why, well, birds are able to fly."

"Umm..." Aurora said. "So how do we change this?"

"We have to find a way," Cynthia explained, "to make the feathers have very, very little air resistance."

"And do we know how?" Aurora asked back.

"By figuring out the best way to bend or twist one, or maybe even putting a few together, or something like that," Maximilian answered.

"How long do we have left!?" Cynthia yelled toward Peter's group.

"You've still got fifty-two minutes! Plenty of time!" Peter replied. "Here, I'll bring you my watch! That way you'll be able to keep track of the time on your own!"

He jogged over and gave his watch to Cynthia. As soon as he got back to the picnic table, he told Neil to start his stopwatch.

"Why?" Neil asked.

"Because we need a way to count down from fifty-two, or, uh, about fifty-one minutes," Peter answered. "And I just lent them mine."

"Here's what I propose," Maximilian said in a logical-sounding tone. "We each grab a third of the feathers and try different ways of bending and twisting them. I figure it might be possible to bend a feather into one of those bizarre things humans have created, which I believe they call rockets? Or are they torpedoes? Anyway, if we can find a way to do that, it should fall quite straight and fast."

"Now that's more like it," Cynthia said, liking the fact that Maximilian was finally being a team player. "And as soon as anyone makes one that looks viable, say something and we will test it out."

Nicola, Neil, Claire, and Zoltan were having a great time chatting away. Bradley and Peter, on the other hand, were both pre-occupied. But their pre-occupations were about two very different things: Peter had asked Neil, "How many minutes left?" so many times now that Neil had just given his watch to Peter. And Bradley was, no doubt, contemplating his *next move* on how to impress Aurora.

Maximilian, Aurora, and Cynthia were really getting into this challenge. Only twenty minutes had elapsed, and they'd come up with some very inventive and creative ways to contort the feathers. Some of their creations even fell quite quickly. Cynthia had produced the best one so far. She had folded one feather exactly in half and then twisted it incredibly tight.

Their fingers were starting to get a little sore, so Aurora proposed that they take a short break and discuss some other options.

"What we haven't tried yet," Cynthia suggested, "is twisting two or three together."

"Interesting idea," Maximilian pondered. "That would make it a little heavier. And if we could twist them tightly enough, that should cut down on the air resistance a lot."

"And it might be best," Aurora suggested, "if we use two short ones and one long one. That way you could use the extra part of the long one to tie knots on both ends. That would hold them together for sure."

Once they decided on which three feathers to

use, Cynthia—the one with the strongest fingers of the three—wound them together so tightly that you heard the shafts of the feathers snap and pop as she did so.

"Looks great!" Maximilian said. "Let's call it our *feather rocket*. Go ahead and give it a try."

Cynthia held the feather rocket and the golf ball at waist level and let go of them at the same time. It was actually a pretty close "race," but unfortunately the golf ball hit the ground first.

"I think we just have to roll it even tighter," Aurora suggested.

"I agree," Maximilian added. He placed it on the picnic table, put a rock on top of it, and rolled the rock back and forth a few times. This caused some of the barbs of the feathers to break off from the shafts. It had become quite a bit tighter, which should equate to a quicker drop.

When they tested it this time, their "finely tuned" feather rocket landed just a split second after the golf ball.

"Close, but no cigar," Peter said under his breath as he watched from a nearby tree which he was hiding behind.

Time was running out for the trio. They only had about ten minutes to go, but no matter how tightly they wound it, they just could not get it to beat the ball to the ground.

"How about a hint!?" Aurora yelled toward Peter, fully aware of where he was hiding.

"A hint?" Peter replied, caught off guard by this unexpected request.

"Peter," Zoltan said loudly from the picnic table. "Come here for a second."

Peter ran back to where Zoltan and the rest of them were sitting.

"We want this to build their camaraderie," Zoltan explained. "I think a hint would be a good thing."

Peter got up and ran back to Maximilian, Aurora, and Cynthia. "Okay," Peter said. "Here's your hint: think location."

"Location?" Maximilian replied. "Location of what?"

"Of you!" Peter replied with a smile. He couldn't say anything more without spelling out the solution for them.

Maximilian, Aurora, and Cynthia sat back down at their picnic table to contemplate the meaning of Peter's hint. They only had about seven minutes left, so they needed to decipher his clue quickly.

"Our location?" Maximilian said. "Is he implying that this task could be completed if we were in a different spot?"

"But where could we go that would make any difference?" Cynthia asked aloud. "I mean, gravity doesn't change based on where you are standing."

"You've got to be kidding me!" Aurora blurted

out with a huge smile on her face. "Follow me! Quick!" She grabbed the golf ball and the feather rocket and started running.

"Where are we going?" Maximilian asked, struggling to catch up to the sprinting Aurora.

"Over there," she said while pointing at the steep hill just beyond the tree line.

Peter and Bradley decided to follow the group, as they wanted to officially witness whether or not they were able to complete the challenge successfully.

"You think they're onto it?" Bradley asked Peter. "You think your clue gave up too much info?"

Claire came running over to join Bradley and Peter, as it was she who had come up with this brilliant puzzle in the first place.

"Five minutes to go!" Peter yelled.

Aurora climbed to the steepest part of the hill. "Watch and learn!" she announced loudly.

She then turned and faced sideways. Since the hill was so steep, this meant her right leg was straight and her left one was bent. Her left foot was at about the same level as her right knee. It looked like she was going to lose her balance.

"I'll do the dropping," she said in a silly voice, "and you all do the watching!"

She held the golf ball in her right hand on her right side and the feather rocket in her left hand on her left side. Both were at waist level.

"I get it!" Maximilian suddenly blurted out.

"Me too!" Cynthia yelled.

Aurora let go of both. Since she was standing sideways on the steep slope of the hill, the golf ball had much further to fall than the feather rocket. They all watched as the feather rocket hit the ground first.

"Well done!" Claire said happily. "I had a feeling one of you'd figure it out eventually."

Peter walked over with his right hand up in the air. Maximilian, Aurora, and Cynthia had no idea what he was trying to communicate to them. Bradley, realizing the trainees were not yet familiar with high-fives, came over and gave a big one to Peter.

Now aware of this new way of celebrating, they all gave numerous high-fives to each other, smiling and laughing the whole time.

"That was so fun!" Cynthia said. "Got any more?"

"Not today," Peter replied. "But we certainly can do something like this again, uh... maybe next Sunday... or possibly the Sunday after that?"

CHAPTER 9

They began walking back toward where Neil, Zoltan, and Nicola were waiting. Peter was smiling on the inside. He had always been fascinated by how strangers or acquaintances could turn into friends so quickly by simply playing some sort of game together.

Since there were six of them in total on the hill, they naturally split up into smaller groups during the walk back to the picnic table. At first, no one noticed that Bradley and Aurora were lagging a fair distance behind, but Claire realized it after a couple minutes. Peter shushed her just as she was about to say something.

"He's in the zone," Peter told her. "Let's leave them alone. I mean, how often do you get the chance to pick up a hot weather god? Can't hurt to let him try, can it?"

"Suppose not," Claire replied.

Bradley had a history of relationships that ended either abruptly, disastrously, or unexpectedly. And another pattern that seemed to be the same was that all of his ex's were attractive, well-dressed, and very concerned about their image. And although Peter had never—and would never—mention this next part to Bradley: all of Bradley's ex-girlfriends were also fairly "dumb and ditzy," to put it politely.

So Peter felt pleased and content that Bradley was currently interested in a highly intelligent woman. But what would a sexy weather god find attractive about a simple human? Anyway, enough with that train of thought...

* * *

"We've heard so many stories about Peter back on Sevlar," Aurora said to Bradley, "but so few about you."

"Well, Petey is the brains behind our team," Bradley replied, sensing that complimenting his younger brother was going to benefit him in his goal to get Aurora to like him more. "I mean, he's one of the smartest people his age in the whole country!"

"That is so cool," Aurora replied. "But I want to know more about *you*, Brad. Or is it Bradley? You know, what makes you tick?"

Bradley carefully contemplated his next move. He knew not only *what* he said next, but also *how* he chose to say it was going to significantly impact his chances with this beautiful young woman.

"As silly as this may sound," he replied, "my answer to that question has changed dramatically over the last three or four months."

"What do you mean?" she asked, eager to hear more.

"Well, and I hope this doesn't make me sound like a *stupid typical* male," he continued. "Back in high school, I only cared about two things: how well I was doing at sports, and how hot my girlfriend was."

"How hot?" she asked, obviously not familiar with the slang.

"*Hot* means beautiful... or sexy, or attractive," he replied nervously. "But then when I started college, which was only about three months ago, it was as if someone switched on my brain for the first time ever. I chose to major in sports science, you know, just because I like sports and I'm good at them. But as soon as I started learning the science behind sports, I just fell in love with the science part of athletics."

"That is so amazing," Aurora said with a twinkle in her eyes.

* * *

Peter, Claire, Maximilian, and Cynthia had rejoined the others and had just finished telling them how Aurora had solved the riddle. Bradley and Aurora were extremely far back now, and they had even stopped walking. No one could hear what they were talking about. But maybe that was for the best...

Bradley noticed everyone was looking their way, so he decided it was time to start moving again.

Once they were within a few meters of the group, Zoltan made an announcement, "Guess what, everyone? We are all heading to Mr. Winchester's now for a big lunch!"

"Mr. Winchester's!?" Peter asked. "But he—"

"No need to worry," Zoltan said confidently. "I visited him last night, and he said he would be happy to host us for lunch today."

"But he's, like, really old," Nicola said, sounding concerned. "That's a lot of people to cook for."

"No need to worry about that either," Zoltan replied. "The arrangement with him is that we will bring all of the food and drinks with us."

"Cool," Bradley said. "But what are we going to buy? And where?"

"Pizza! Pizza! Pizza!" Neil chanted while jumping up and down like an immature boy.

"Would you five mind doing the shopping?" Zoltan asked, handing Bradley an envelope with cash in it.

"Not at all," Bradley replied while glancing down briefly at the money. "But where did you get this from?"

"Let's just say," Maximilian answered quickly, "that the lead weather gods gave us all a lot of money to bring back for Zoltan. You know, kind of like, uh, what do you call it on Earth... an, uh, expense account? You know, to cover any costs involved during our training."

"But how did they get *cash*?" Peter asked.

"Oh, Peter," Maximilian said, laughing off the question. "Always the inquisitor. I think I'm beginning to really like you."

Bradley handed Peter the cash and started walking to his car. "You know my track record with losing things," he laughed. "You're in charge of the money, Petey."

Peter could tell by the thickness of the envelope that there was way, way more than would be needed for a bunch of pizzas and a few bottles of soft drinks.

CHAPTER 10

On the drive to the pizza shop, Peter started counting through the money in the envelope. Every bill was a ten, and he counted forty in total. His second count reconfirmed his first: they had just been given the sum of four hundred dollars. This was at least three times more than they actually required.

When Peter told everyone how much they had received, they didn't believe him at first. But one glance at Peter's face, which had that "I'm not making this up" look on it, immediately convinced them.

"Let's go to that place on Third Avenue. You know, Antonio's," Neil suggested.

"Of course that's where we're headed!" Bradley replied. "I mean we are definitely NOT going to one of those cheap pizza shops where they barely put any toppings on, and then either overcook or undercook them."

"And while we are waiting for them to make

the pizzas," Claire added, "why don't some of us go to the supermarket across the street and get the snacks and drinks?"

"I love it when a plan comes together," Bradley said in a deep voice, imitating a phrase he must have gotten from some TV show. "But while you guys are doing that, I have to make a quick pit stop somewhere."

Everyone in the car suddenly went silent. Something about the tone of Bradley's voice was odd and eerie.

"What are you guys acting so weird about?" Bradley asked. "All I need to do is go and get gas!"

The other four looked instantly relieved. They were expecting to hear Bradley say something a lot more serious or bizarre.

"And Petey," he continued, "score me some of that money for gas. Because technically, I *need* the gas to drive us to Mr. Winchester's, right?"

Peter passed Bradley one of the ten-dollar bills.

"Come on, give me at least twenty bucks," Bradley pleaded.

"No way, Brad," Peter replied. "We are not going to take advantage of this. You get ten for gas and not a penny more."

"Cheapskate," Bradley joked while pulling into the pizza shop parking lot. "Alright, jump out here everyone; I'll be back as soon as I can."

"And please ask the gas station attendant for a

receipt," Peter said before getting out. "I want proof that you spent the entire ten on fuel."

"Aren't you lucky?" Claire said to Bradley. "It's like you have two moms!"

* * *

Twenty-five minutes later, with five fresh pizzas, half a dozen big bottles of pop, and four bags of chips, they started the drive to Mr. Winchester's home. Bradley told Neil, who was now sitting in the passenger seat, to open up the glove compartment and pick a CD.

"Dude," Neil replied. "You just leave the tune selection to the Neilster!"

"Stop! New rule, effectively immediately!" Bradley announced with a big smile. "The next person who says the word *Neilster* is walking the rest of the way."

"I second that idea!" Nicola said right away.

"Me too!" Claire agreed.

"Me three!" Peter said, putting up his hand for some high-fives.

Neil turned around to look at everyone in the back seat. "Are you guys trying to tell me," he asked, "that I've grown out of that nickname?"

"That would be impossible," Peter replied, "as you never grew into it in the first place!"

Everyone, Neil included, burst into laughter.

"Dudes," Neil said with a grin, "I'm hurt. But man, why didn't someone tell me this, like, years ago? I thought my nickname was cool!"

Everyone was still laughing too hard to reply.

"Well then," Neil continued, "I will *temporarily* retire that nickname."

"Temporarily?" Bradley asked. "Why not permanently?"

"Never put all your eggs in one basket," Neil replied.

Peter was laughing so hard now that his stomach muscles were starting to hurt and his face was beet red. Neil had just done what Peter's dad did all too frequently: completely misuse a saying, without having a clue that he'd done so.

The drive to Mr. Winchester's was turning out to be so much more entertaining than they ever could have imagined.

CHAPTER 11

When they pulled into Mr. Winchester's driveway, he was sitting on the front porch soaking up the sunshine. He did have a coat on, but it was a very thin-looking one, and definitely too light for such a cold day.

"You must be freezing?" Nicola asked as she ran up the front stairs and gave him a big hug.

"Suppose I might be," he answered with a giggle, "but I'm so old now I wouldn't even notice."

Claire also gave him a hug, but the boys decided to use high-fives instead. For some reason, boys this age weren't comfortable with the man hugging man thing.

"So when is this weather god crew due to arrive?" Mr. Winchester asked. "I can't wait to meet them."

"Dunno," Neil answered. "We figured they'd be here by now."

"Yeah," Bradley added. "It's not like they have to use cars to get from *A* to *B*."

"Hmm..." Mr. Winchester said while rubbing his chin. "Anyway, I'm sure they'll arrive soon."

"Alright everyone," Claire announced loudly. "You're all more than welcome to continue chatting in the cold, but I'm heading inside. My fingers are freezing."

"I'm with you!" Nicola said quickly.

The boys and Mr. Winchester agreed as well, and quickly followed suit.

It looked as if Mr. Winchester had prepared his home for a huge holiday feast. He had even somehow managed to get the kitchen table into the dining room. With the two tables together, they easily had enough space for ten. He had also put out the placemats, plates, napkins, cutlery, and salt and pepper shakers. Plus he had added a few candles—which weren't lit yet—to give his plain and simple home a little more ambiance.

"Mr. Winchester," Peter asked, "how did you manage to haul that heavy kitchen table in here?"

"Yeah," Bradley added. "Have you been pumping iron behind our backs?"

"Afraid not, Bradley," Mr. Winchester said while slowly sitting down in his rocking chair. "My weight-lifting days, or whatever you young folks call it now, stopped long before you were even in grade school." He rocked back and forth a couple times, and then continued, "Actually, when Zoltan came over to ask me to host this gathering, he used a little bit of his supernatural powers to move the table."

"I see," Peter replied, relieved to have his inquiry answered. (Peter despised the part of his brain that always latched onto unanswered questions and obsessed over them endlessly.)

"So how do we decide who sits where?" Claire asked. "I mean, it would be best if we mixed everyone up, right? That way we'd be talking to them instead of just to each other."

Claire was, once again, using her experience as the former volleyball team captain when making that suggestion. She obviously knew what was required to help people break the ice.

"I'm going to make little name cards," she continued, "and put them on the plates."

"Assigned seating, eh?" Mr. Winchester laughed from his rocking chair. "Quite the organized operation!"

"You bet!" Claire answered.

"There's plenty of paper and pens in the third drawer of that desk in the corner," Mr. Winchester said. "Knock yourself out!"

"Awesome," she replied. "I'll get on it."

* * *

"Wonder what's taking them so long?" Peter asked, looking first at his watch, and then out the window again.

"No kidding, eh?" Neil added. "They could have easily *tornadoed* their way here in an instant!"

"Think they got lost?" Bradley asked. "Want

me to drive around and—"

"There's no need to do anything like that," Mr. Winchester said. "Let them take their sweet time. The pizzas are in the oven, so they'll still taste like they're fresh. And in case you all forgot, there's an old man in a rocking chair who'd love to hear how you are all doing."

The sofa wasn't big enough to seat five, so Bradley effortlessly hauled over two chairs from the dining room table. Everyone sat down and started watching Mr. Winchester rock slowly back and forth.

"This isn't grade school," the old man laughed. "There is no rule about who has to speak first. Just fill me in on what's new."

Although the ensuing conversation felt a little unnatural at first, within a few minutes, everyone was chatting and laughing away. And before they knew it, they had diverged from current up-dates to reminiscing about the past. The more they talked, the more the volume of laughter increased.

Ding-dong

Everyone kind of froze right after hearing the doorbell. They had been so relaxed for the last little while that they had almost forgotten about the actual purpose of today's get-together.

"You're not waiting for me to struggle out of

this rocking chair to get the door, are you?" Mr. Winchester asked his young friends.

"Sorry," Peter said, quickly walking over to open the door for the special guests.

While he did that, Bradley helped Mr. Winchester out of his chair, so that he would be standing when the three young weather-gods-to-be came to shake his hand.

As soon as Zoltan had removed his boots, he walked directly to Mr. Winchester and gave the old man a long hug.

"Don't squeeze too hard," Mr. Winchester joked. "Old guys like me break pretty easily!"

This joke seemed to make the atmosphere a little less tense for Maximilian, Aurora, and Cynthia to come up to shake hands with him.

* * *

The meal and all of the various conversations going on were great. Zoltan had had pizza a few times, but Maximilian, Aurora, and Cynthia had never even heard of it. And when they said that they'd never eaten anything with their hands before, it was quite an entertaining task to watch.

Once everyone was stuffed to the gills, Neil stood up and announced that he and Claire would do all the clean-up.

Mr. Winchester then suggested they retire to the living room.

"So, Leonardo," Aurora said. "Oh, I'm sorry, is it okay if I call you that?"

Mr. Winchester chuckled. "It's completely alright," he replied. "I can't even remember the last time someone so pretty called me by my name."

"We are so keen to hear," Aurora continued, "how you managed to create all those puzzles for Zoltan for so long. He told us how hard, complicated, and confusing they were. But he also said that despite the high level of difficulty, he managed to solve every single one."

"Did he now??" Mr. Winchester replied, looking over at Zoltan.

"Sure," Cynthia added. "Or at least that's what he told us."

"Hold on," Zoltan said, pausing and clearing his throat. "I didn't tell you I solved *every single one*."

"Yes, you did," Maximilian said. "I specifically remember you saying that he never outsmarted you."

Mr. Winchester's grin grew. "A little too embarrassed to admit I got you that one time, eh?" he said to Zoltan. "Come on now, don't you want them to hear about the one that stumped you?"

Sensing Zoltan's discomfort, Bradley quickly changed the subject. He wanted to divert the conversation away from Zoltan's "one and only" incomplete challenge.

"What *we* don't get," Bradley said, "is why everyone on Sevlar is so obsessed with puzzles and riddles. What's with that?"

"No kidding," Neil added. "Sevlar sounds like a world full of Peters!"

That got everyone laughing.

"Please, not that!" Nicola said mid-laugh. "One Peter is all we can handle!"

When the laughter had finally subsided, the six earthlings were waiting to hear the answer to Bradley's question. They had all assumed that Zoltan would be the one to answer, but it was actually Maximilian who spoke up.

"The reason is quite simple," Maximilian began. "On Sevlar, we begin doing puzzles and riddles from a young age. Very young. Think of it this way: Little Earth kids go to the park. Little Sevlar kids do riddles. And then when we are being schooled, the whole focus is on developing our problem-solving skills."

"You mean," Bradley asked, "you don't study math or science or stuff like that?"

"Of course we study those as well," Maximilian replied. "But education is geared at giving us minds capable of analyzing and solving problems." He paused and looked at his audience. "Well, I can see this is getting boring already, but—"

"Boring?" Peter said, interrupting Maximilian. "No way! A world full of people who all love puzzles? An education system based around problem-solving?"

"That would be your dream world, eh Petey?"

Bradley commented.

Peter recognized that he now had a rare opportunity that would score him some points with his girlfriend. "If they'd let me take Nik there," he proudly announced. "Then it would be perfect!"

"You little Casanova!" Claire laughed, elbowing Peter. "Don't tell me you've already made plans to get married?"

* * *

The luncheon had been a huge success. Both groups had learned a lot about each other, and everyone felt much more comfortable being in the same room.

Mr. Winchester had originally estimated the whole affair would last no longer than ninety minutes, but his four weather god guests had spent almost three hours in his home. Very soon, it would start getting dark outside. Mr. Winchester was thanked graciously as they departed, and all four told the old man they couldn't wait to see him again.

The five teenagers were in a giddy mood as they also put their coats and shoes on. Bradley went outside first, so he could start the car and give it a chance to warm up.

Mr. Winchester, on the other hand, looked as if he was worried about something. He rocked slowly back and forth, staring at, well, nothing...

"Everything okay?" Nicola asked him. "You

must be exhausted. We should've ended things earlier today."

"Oh, it's nothing like that," he replied. "It's just, I, uh… I can't really put my finger on it."

"What do you mean?" Peter asked, realizing Mr. Winchester had something he needed to get off his chest.

"I've always been quite a worrier, so I'm sure it's all just in my head," he went on. "But a few times today while we were eating, and even a couple of times while seated in the living room, I noticed the three trainees occasionally making eye contact with each other.

"What's weird about that?" Bradley asked. "I thought eye contact was considered a good thing."

"Well, it is…" he replied awkwardly. "I mean, it *usually* is. But something just didn't seem a hundred percent natural about theirs… it was, and as I said before, I'm sure I am just being paranoid, it was like they were coordinating their answers."

"Mr. Winchester," the concerned Peter said. "You know I take the gold medal when it comes to worrying. I didn't notice anything."

"Thanks, Peter," he said softly. "Just hearing that will help me sleep a little better tonight."

CHAPTER 12

After finishing the last of his final exams at three o'clock on Friday, Bradley felt like shouting "Yes!" at the top of his lungs as he walked toward his car in the college parking lot. He had studied very hard for all seven classes this term and was confident that his exam grades would reflect his efforts. He had an 80% or higher in all of his classes going into the finals, so his odds of getting straight A's in his first term at college were quite good.

"Hi, Brad," a soft voice said from behind him as he was preparing to unlock the car door.

Bradley was sure he had heard that voice somewhere before, but couldn't pinpoint who it was without twisting his head around to look. He was blown away to see Aurora standing by the back bumper of his car.

"H... hi," he replied, in what seemed to be a very uncharacteristic display of nervousness. "Wh... what are you doing here? Sorry, that came out wrong. Aren't you supposed to be busy, you know, dealing with weather stuff?"

"Actually," she replied with a smile, "Zoltan gave us the afternoon off today. I think he could see that we were all pretty drained."

"Oh," Bradley replied.

"Well," she continued quickly, "we weren't really that drained. We were just getting a little tired. Actually, *bored* would be a better word to describe it." She started blushing a bit. "Anyway, I figured I would come and find you, and see if you'd be able to, I don't know, show me around a little?"

Bradley had asked out or been asked out by tons of girls over the past six and a half years. His well-trained instincts were telling him this girl liked him.

"Let me think," he said very nonchalantly, preparing a little lie he expected would impress her. "I was planning to work out this afternoon, and then drop by Thomas' party tonight. But..." He paused to add some drama. "I can skip the gym once in a while, right? Plus the party will probably be lame anyway."

"Hold on," she giggled. "Does that mean you *can* or *can't* take me somewhere?"

"What I am saying, young lady," Bradley said while opening the passenger door for her, "is that I will be your personal chauffeur. Oops, I guess you've probably never heard that word." He laughed. "That just means your driver and guide, I guess. And I'll be taking you to all of the coolest places I know."

"Really?" she said as Bradley got ready to close the door for her. "Wow!"

Bradley smugly grinned to himself as he walked behind the car to go back to the driver's side. He knew the next few hours would decide whether or not this would turn into a relationship. Based on her positive reactions so far, he had already convinced himself that things with this beautiful lady were indeed heading in the right direction.

* * *

They started off with coffees at a funky little cafe that let the patrons make requests about which songs were played. There wasn't a DJ or anything like that, just shelves upon shelves of CDs. All you had to do was take one down, hand it to the owner, and tell her which song or songs you wanted to hear.

Shortly after being introduced to her first-ever cup of coffee, and music like nothing she had ever heard back on Sevlar, they got back into Bradley's car and headed toward the five-pin bowling alley in Stoneburg. Stoneburg also had a fancy new bowling alley, with only ten-pin lanes. But the older five-pin place was popular enough with the regulars that it somehow managed to stay open. This bowling alley was Bradley's *go-to spot* for every first date. There was never anyone their age there, plus the bowling itself always led to laughs, high-fives, and occasionally a few celebratory hugs. No one knew how to pull off a first date as well as Bradley.

Once they'd finished their game and a milkshake, they drove back to Clearville, to a little Mexican place on Fourth Avenue. The owner knew Bradley quite well since his son and Bradley had played basketball together in high school. The food was delicious and cheap, and even more importantly, they had two semi-private tables. Bradley, thinking ahead, had phoned before they started bowling and reserved one of those tables for tonight.

They hadn't even been at the restaurant for twenty minutes when Aurora reached across the table and took Bradley's hand. "Brad," she said with a sparkle in her eyes. "You're so different from the men where I am from. It's like you know what I'm thinking."

"Know what you're thinking?" Bradley smiled. "Afraid I'm not a mind reader. Wish I were, but—"

"Brad," she said, cutting him off and squeezing his hand even tighter. "Maximilian, Cynthia, and Zoltan can never know about us going out today. Never. They'd send me back to Sevlar instantly."

"Why?" he asked. "They have no right to tell you who you can and can't hang out with."

"No, technically they don't," she answered. "And there are no guidelines regarding what's considered *acceptable* while we are here. But the lead weather gods gave Zoltan the authority to send home anyone who does anything he deems inappropriate."

"Your secret's safe with me," he said with a wink.

They finished up their evening at another one of Bradley's favorite date spots. Before driving there, he stopped by a convenience store and picked up two large hot chocolates. Then they made the short drive to the area before the landing strip of the tiny Clearville Airport, which was a town park with a few picnic tables and park benches. No planes took off or landed after six, so this place was always empty in the evenings. That meant they would have complete privacy.

As soon as they were out of the car and heading toward one of the benches, Aurora wrapped her arm around Bradley's. This girl certainly wasn't shy.

They sipped their hot chocolates in the cold, sitting so close to each other that there was no air space between them. His years of dating experience, plus his talent for reading people, told Bradley that the opportunity for a first kiss was presenting itself. He leaned in and gave her a soft, quick kiss, and then pulled back to see her reaction. The expression on her face told Bradley that the little peck had been exactly the right thing to do.

"I don't have a curfew," Bradley said, "but I should be getting home soon. School is out for the Christmas holiday, but track and field practice doesn't take a break between terms. I've gotta be there at seven o'clock sharp tomorrow morning."

She patted him lightly several times on the chest. "No problem, off you go, big guy," she said. "We don't want you to do anything that could raise suspicions about us. Oh... and unless you've already got plans for tomorrow, do you think we could continue this date once your practice is done?"

That question caught Bradley off-guard, but he made sure to respond in a positive (but not excessively eager) way. "Yeah, sounds good to me," he said cool and collectively. "So where should I drop you off tonight?"

She leaned in close to his left ear. "I'm a weather god, in case you forgot," she whispered. "I can go where I need to go on my own. But I think I'll just sit here by myself for a little while. This bench has just become a spot with special meaning for me."

"You sure?" he asked again.

"Positive," she replied. "But before you go, I have a little favor to ask."

"A favor?" Bradley inquired.

She leaned in close again and whispered in his ear.

Bradley turned to look at her. "That's it?" he asked.

"Yes," she replied.

"Should be no problem at all," he said while starting to walk to his car.

"You're the best!" she said just as Bradley closed the car door. "See you tomorrow!"

"I wonder if all girls from Sevlar are like this?" Bradley asked himself while driving back toward the highway. "If they are, I've gotta find a way to visit there some day!"

CHAPTER 13

With Bradley gone to track and field practice, and Sophia off at a ballet recital with his mom, that left only Peter and his dad home on Saturday morning.

"Hey, Pete," his dad announced in a loud voice as he walked into the kitchen where Peter was eating breakfast. "Your mother has given you and me a job to do today. And you know that when she gives someone a job to do, it better get done."

"Great," Peter answered sarcastically. "What is it?"

"We have been placed in charge of putting up the outdoor Christmas lights," his dad said.

"Really?" Peter replied. "I thought she had decided against putting them up this year. And isn't it a little late? I mean, other homes have had them up for weeks."

"What we think about this is completely irrelevant," his dad explained. "If *Her Highness* orders them to go up today, then that's what has to happen."

Peter laughed at the way his dad would make these silly comments about his mom when she wasn't around, but wouldn't dare do such a thing if she were at home.

His dad had already hauled in the two boxes from the garage which contained the outdoor Christmas light sets. Each set was basically just a long electrical cord with a colored light every twenty-five centimeters or so. Their first task was to plug in each set—of which there were four in total—in order to spot the bulbs that were burnt out and needed replacing.

"But dad, we haven't bought any replacement bulbs," Peter said.

"Pete," his dad smiled, pointing at the dining room table. "You know your mother. She bought eight packs of replacement bulbs yesterday. Two of each color."

"Does she ever forget anything?" Peter asked.

"Forget stuff?" his dad replied. "Nope. That's my job."

The bulb replacing was the easiest of part today's operation, as it could be done in the comfort of their warm living room.

* * *

When all four sets were ready to go, they put on their heavy winter clothes, got the folding ladder and extension ladder from the garage, and headed outside to get their task over and done with.

Neither Peter nor his dad had to ask about which set went where, as they had been well-labeled by his mom. One had "outdoor tree" on it, one had "garage," one had "living room window and front door," and the last one had "upper gutter."

They decided to start with the easy ones first and leave the worst one—the upper gutter one—until the end.

When the first three were all up nicely, Peter's dad set up the extension ladder in just the right position to get started on the final set of lights. He figured he could put the cord into three or four clips at a time before he'd have to climb down and move the ladder over a little.

"Hold it tight, boy," his dad instructed, getting ready to head up the ladder for the first time. "Not just with your hands."

"Wait," Peter said suddenly. "Uh… I'll go up."

"Nah, I'll be fine," his dad said back.

Peter hadn't made the offer because he was worried about his dad's safety, it had been for a completely different, and quite selfish reason: he had just remembered about the light he had rigged up in the chimney—the one he used when he needed to call Zoltan. If he let his dad go up the ladder, his dad would surely spot the cord that came from the chimney to just outside Peter's bedroom window. And then a full "investigation" was bound to happen.

"No dad, I got this," he said. "You've done most of the hard stuff today. It's only fair that I do this part. Plus, I've got way better balance than you."

His dad was obviously not really that concerned about who was in charge of each task. His only real concern was that it got done, and done properly. (They both knew the tongue-lashing they would get if they did a sloppy job.)

Luckily for the both of them, the plastic clips which Peter's dad had attached to gutter a few years back were all still intact. That meant all they had to do was simply clip the cable in. Peter was using Bradley's hi-tech cross-country ski gloves, which were really thin but also warm. And his multiple trips up and down the ladder had gotten his blood pumping enough to prevent his hands from feeling cold.

* * *

Job now complete to a level that would definitely satisfy *the boss*, Peter's dad said, "Alright, let's hope there isn't a message waiting for us on the answering machine with another chore."

"No kidding," Peter agreed, as they both started peeling off the multiple layers of clothing they'd needed while outside.

"You want a tea?" his dad asked as they hung up their jackets and put their gloves and winter caps back into the plastic box labeled "gloves and hats."

"I hate tea," Peter replied. "You know that."

"How about a coffee, then?" his dad asked.

"Coffee?" Peter laughed. "That stuff tastes like tar."

"Try telling your mother that," his dad said. "She drinks five or six cups of that stuff a day."

Peter went up to his room. Unlike his dad, he didn't need a hot drink to warm himself up. Well, he wanted one, but he still remembered that awful wintery day when he had scalded his tongue on hot chocolate at age nine. And the *paranoid little boy inside him* couldn't convince the logical fifteen-year-old to forget about it.

He lay down on his bed and kind of zoned out. He didn't even start staring at the stucco ceiling; instead, he just moved his eyes around the room, without really stopping to focus on anything. It took him ages to notice something he should have spotted straight away: there was a leaf and a note taped to the outside of his window.

"What the...?" Peter said, feeling his anxiety start to ramp up. He began to take deep breaths in an effort to calm his nerves and settle down. This seemed to help a little, especially when he forecast that the note was likely just a request from Zoltan to make another puzzle for tomorrow.

"Yeah, that's probably all he wants," Peter told himself. "It's just a puzzle request."

He slid the cold window open, reached his arm outside and took off the leaf and the note. He chucked the leaf in the garbage can beside his desk and then lay back down on his bed. He got ready to check the message, already guessing about its contents.

Peter started reading the note and then suddenly gulped. Twice. "Okay, this is weird," he said to himself. "Really, really weird."

He folded the note, put it in his back pocket, and started heading for the front door. This was the first time Zoltan had ever used phrases like *of great urgency* or *as soon as you see this* in a note. The last part of the note told Peter where Zoltan was currently waiting for him. Their usual rendezvous point was too far away to get to in this cold weather, so Zoltan had picked a spot in a small park less than two hundred meters from Peter's front door.

Peter's arms couldn't manage to put on his outdoor gear as fast as his mind was ordering them to. He almost fell over twice while bending down to tie up his boots. As much as he hated to admit it, he was panicking. But this time, maybe his panic was warranted.

"Dad!" he yelled as he was about to open the door. "I'm going to Neil's!"

"Gotcha," his dad replied. "Tell the Neilster that I said hi!"

CHAPTER 14

Peter wanted to get to the park as quickly as he could, but knew the fresh snow on the sidewalk—which had been falling since yesterday afternoon—combined with his poor co-ordination skills, was likely a recipe for disaster if he were to run. So he elected to compromise and did a very awkward-looking version of speed walking instead.

When he got to the park, he saw Zoltan sitting quite peacefully on one of the benches, reading a thick, hardcover book.

"Zoltan!" Peter said loudly as he got closer. "Sorry I didn't spot your note earlier. I wasn't in my room this morning at all. I was outside helping my dad put up the Christmas lights."

"You have nothing to apologize for, Peter," Zoltan said calmly. "And since I visited that big library on Leeds Street a few days ago, where I borrowed this fascinating book, I've had plenty to occupy my mind."

"How did you do that?" Peter asked. "You can't get a library card without having an address."

"True," he answered. "Actually, I went with Leonardo, and he technically borrowed the book for me. Now, sorry to change subjects so abruptly, but there is something we need to discuss."

"I gathered that much from the language in your note," Peter replied. "What's going on?"

"First, please have a seat," Zoltan said, motioning for Peter to sit down beside him. "And before I start, I think I should point out to you that I occasionally catastrophize. So everything I am about to say may simply be my mind creating negative outcomes."

"Gotcha," Peter said. "I can certainly relate to that. No judging here."

"Then allow me to begin," Zoltan continued. "The specific thing concerning me is related to yesterday afternoon and evening. On Fridays, I have all three trainees come back from their respective continents. That way I can check in with them on how things went over the past week and then we can work on a new technique or two. But something was off yesterday. They all showed up a little early, something which had never happened before. Okay... I guess *that* part wasn't too strange. Anyway, they were talking away as I approached them, but the instant they noticed me, they completely hushed up. When I casually asked what their conversation was about, they just laughed it off and changed the subject. Once the weekly check-in was complete and we had finished lunch, I noticed all three were very reluctant to put any effort into practicing the new technique I had just demonstrated. I decided to give them the benefit of the doubt, and just put their lackluster effort down to tiredness."

"I know I shouldn't interrupt," Peter said. "But in all likelihood, they were just tired. I mean, they just spent four consecutive days, in separate parts of the globe, battling weather troubles."

"True," Zoltan continued. "I also considered that possibility myself. Now, where was I? Oh... so I elected to give them the afternoon off. Not only that, but I also told them to take Saturday off, too. Plus, I said I would talk with you about creating a Sunday puzzle for them. That news, or at least the possibility of it, did appear to raise their spirits somewhat."

"Sorry again, Zoltan," Peter interjected. "But so far nothing seems weird or out of place to me."

"It's what occurred next that's troubling me the most," Zoltan went on. "I was a little worried about them, so at about half past seven yesterday evening, I went by to see how they were doing. And get this, no one was there. I waited for a good hour or so, but not even one of them returned."

"If you gave them Friday night and all day Saturday off," Peter said, "then they probably decided to go out and party. Or at least go out and explore the town. I mean, they haven't been on Earth for long."

"Also true," Zoltan nodded. "But there's more. I knew I wouldn't be able to sleep with all this worry, so I went to Mr. Winchester's house. Basically, I wanted to tell him the exact same thing I just told you."

"And did he react any differently than me?" Peter asked.

"No, not at all," Zoltan replied. "Just like you are doing now, he listened and then told me I was worrying about nothing. It was when I was *leaving* that I got the real shock."

"Shock?" Peter asked.

"Yes," Zoltan answered. "You know there was a light snowfall on Friday afternoon. Not heavy, maybe two centimeters or so. After I had thanked Leonardo, closed the front door, and went to head down the steps, I noticed there were two fresh pairs of footprints that went up the steps and toward the living room window. But there were no footprints leading away from the window."

"So you think that two of the three came here, spied on you from outside the window, and then used their supernatural powers to depart, don't you?" Peter asked.

"Yes, that's exactly what I'm thinking," he replied.

"I'd be lying if I said nothing sounds odd," Peter admitted, "but I wouldn't say it warrants too much worrying yet. For all we know, they could have been trying to plan some kind of surprise for you."

"Hmm..." Zoltan mumbled. "I suppose it's theoretically possible, but..."

"Tell you what," Peter suggested. "I will make a Sunday puzzle for them to do, and bring Nik along with me. She, if anyone, knows how to coax information out of people without them knowing. If something is up, she'll be able to find out."

"Excellent plan," Zoltan replied happily. "Thank you, Peter."

"Hey man," Peter said, putting his hand up for a high-five. "We are on the same team now. And that's what friends are for!"

CHAPTER 15

Peter and Zoltan's high five then somehow morphed into a handshake that seemed to go on for an eternity. When Zoltan finally released his hand, Peter smiled at him and turned around to start heading back home.

"And Peter," he said after Peter was already about five meters away, "it doesn't need to be something too complex. I don't want you to waste an entire Saturday afternoon because of me and my worries."

"Okay!" Peter said back. Today's rendezvous with Zoltan made Peter realize that even weather gods could be excessive worriers, and something about that fact actually comforted him a little.

* * *

Peter was planning to ask Bradley to drive him and Nicola tomorrow, but Bradley was gone when Peter returned home.

"Bradley out of the house before noon on a Saturday?" he said to himself. "That's gotta be a first. He must have a special track practice or something. Anyway, guess I'll check *option B* then."

By option B, Peter was referring to Neil. Neil was his only friend who had already completed the driver training course and successfully passed the driver's test. Hopefully, Neil would be able to borrow his mom's car tomorrow to drive them. And by *them*, of course, he meant Claire would be included too.

"Neil, it's me," Peter said into the phone when Neil finally picked it up after six rings.

"Yo, the Petester! What's up, dude?" Neil asked. "It's not like you to phone me up out of the blue. Well, unless you need help with something..."

"C'mon, that's not completely true," Peter said hesitantly. Although it wasn't completely true, it was pretty close. It wasn't that Peter *used* Neil or anything like that, it was just that Peter had always been a very solitary kid. He was completely happy and content to think up, create, and do puzzles and games on his own. So he rarely ever felt the desire to phone up friends.

Peter explained his situation and asked about the possibility of Neil borrowing his mom's car to drive them. Neil told Peter to hold on a second while he went downstairs to ask his mom. Less than a minute later, he was back on the line.

"You have yourselves a driver!" Neil proudly announced.

"Awesome," Peter replied. "I owe you one."

"No, you don't," Neil replied while giggling a little. "You owe *my mom* one. And what you owe has already been decided: as soon as we get back tomorrow, you and I are going to be putting up the outdoor Christmas lights at our house."

Peter forced out a happy-sounding reply. "Cool," he said. "I suppose I'm becoming somewhat of an expert *Christmas light putter-upper*. My dad and I just did ours this morning."

He regretted that comment the instant it came out. Not the "expert" part, but the "dad" part. Neil's dad, who Peter had met a couple of times when he was younger, had divorced Neil's mom and run off with his secretary a couple of years ago. And not only had he left his wife for a younger woman, but he had also chosen to have nothing to do with Neil anymore. Neil hadn't heard from his dad since that unforgettable day two and a half years ago when his mom had to tell him that his dad had left.

"Sorry," Peter said nervously into the phone. "I... uh... didn't mean to..."

"Petey," Neil interrupted in a happy tone. "It is what it is, man. I've got the best mom in the entire world. The entire universe, actually! I consider myself lucky."

After hanging up, Peter quickly called Nicola and said he really needed her help getting a puzzle ready for tomorrow. Nicola offered to help, but only until about four or so, as she had the five to ten o'clock shift tonight. But hey, a few hours of help was certainly better than none at all!

CHAPTER 16

Peter was planning on getting his older brother up to speed on everything that afternoon or evening, but Bradley still hadn't come home by the time Peter went up to his room at ten thirty. Bradley didn't have a curfew, but there was an unwritten agreement with his parents that he would never stay out past midnight. Any later than that was considered "far too late" by his mom. Bradley had broken his curfew a ridiculous number of times back in high school, but since starting college a few months ago, he rarely ever stayed out late.

But after thinking it through a bit more, Peter figured that Bradley really didn't need to know what was going on right away. He'd just tell him the next time an opportunity presented itself.

* * *

The next morning, as Peter walked by Bradley's bedroom door, he put his ear up against it to make sure Bradley had actually come home.

Sure enough, Bradley was snoring away, at a volume that would certainly hurt your ears if you were in the same room as him.

* * *

Bradley's snoring took Peter's mind quickly back to the days when their family lived in a small bungalow, which had been big enough (and cheap enough) until his younger sister Sophia was born. After she arrived into the world, Peter and Bradley were put in a room together in bunk beds and baby Sophia got her own room.

Peter was relegated to the top bunk, as his parents decided that the elder of the two had "first choice." This seemed to make sense, since Peter's bedtime was earlier than Bradley's. (If Bradley had chosen the top, then he would have unintentionally woken Peter up every time he climbed into bed...)

Peter was too young to remember things vividly, but the one thing he would never forget was the awful snoring that emanated from his older brother in the bottom bunk. According to both Bradley and their parents, Peter originally thought Bradley was wide awake and "fake snoring" just to bother his little brother. But when he climbed down to check things out, it was one hundred percent clear that Bradley was sound asleep.

When Peter had asked his parents about it, they said Bradley had been a big snorer, even as a baby. Apparently, when his mom consulted their family doctor about this, the doctor had told her that babies couldn't snore. Peter's mom hated it when people doubted her, so she rocked baby Bradley in her arms until he fell asleep in the doctor's waiting room. And once the loud snoring began, the receptionist went and asked the doctor to come and hear for himself. The middle-aged doctor was nothing less than astonished. "How can such a cute little guy make such a huge and horrible noise?" the doctor had joked.

After being referred to an ear, nose and throat specialist in Stoneburg, who was equally shocked by Bradley's snoring, a full examination revealed that there was absolutely nothing wrong with Bradley's throat or airways.

So poor Peter tried everything: earplugs, covering his head with pillows, sleeping under his covers, and various other methods. But no matter what he did, Bradley's snoring was always overpowering enough that it kept Peter from sleeping.

Then (and this is what he was told, as he doesn't actually remember any of this) Peter decided to take matters into his own hands. Every time Bradley's snoring got too loud to bear, Peter leaned over the edge of the top bunk, pillow in hand, and whacked Bradley in the face until the snoring ceased. It was effective in that it quickly put a stop to the noise, but the snoring always started up again, sometimes within minutes.

* * *

Peter giggled as he tiptoed down to the kitchen, imagining what life was going to be like for Bradley's future wife. He continued smugly laughing while eating breakfast. He kept creating images of Bradley's *darling* whacking him over and over with a pillow.

Peter checked his watch and realized he was ready way too early again: a habit his doctor referred to as "obsessive-compulsive." But official diagnosis aside, Peter was a worrier, and worriers never want to be late.

Neil said he'd roll by to pick up Peter at eight thirty, and it was currently 7:14. He knew his mom would be up soon and wanting her morning coffee fix, so he pushed the "ON" button on the coffee maker. This simple task, which was always appreciated, was something that his dad just never seemed to figure out how to do. His dad was a genius in so many respects, but a moron in others. He'd heard his mom say, so many times, "Stephen, all you have to do is push this button when you come into the kitchen to make your breakfast."

It wasn't that Peter's dad didn't feel like turning on the coffee maker. It was just that despite being the most social and likable person in the whole town, he was notoriously forgetful. Or at least that was the excuse he used...

With over seventy minutes to kill, Peter decided to make good use of his time and started reading the novel which he needed to finish before writing a book report due on Wednesday.

* * *

The book was not as boring as Peter had expected, so he managed to get a reasonable amount of enjoyment out of the hundred-odd pages he read through. This made time fly by, and before he knew it, it was time to put on his outdoor gear and wait just inside the front door for Neil to arrive.

CHAPTER 17

Neil leaned on the horn as he approached Peter's driveway, which was completely unnecessary—and also a little rude and inconsiderate, considering the time of day—since Peter had promised to be waiting and watching through the window next to the front door.

"Yo, the Petester!" Neil said loudly when Peter hopped in the back seat. That was now the second time in two days he'd been called that by Neil. He didn't like this new nickname at all. But since he was extremely grateful that Neil was driving them today, he chose not to complain.

"Hi, Pete," said Claire. "Sorry about the horn. I tried to pull his hand off it as soon as he started. He probably woke up a few of your neighbors."

Peter pointed at his living room window, where his mom, still in her nightgown, was staring at Neil and wagging her finger back and forth. "No biggie," Peter replied. "But don't pull a repeat performance of that when we get to Nik's."

After picking up Nicola, the foursome started the short drive to Meeks Park. It was a chilly morning, and there was not a cloud in the sky. They'd want to find a picnic table in the sun to sit at while Maximilian, Aurora, and Cynthia tackled their puzzle.

"Where's Brad?" Claire asked. "I figured he'd want to come today for sure."

"No kidding," Nicola added. "He's obviously got the hots for Aurora."

"Actually," Peter said, "I was trying to invite him along, but he was out from before I woke up yesterday until after I went to bed last night. Currently he's snoring away in his room. I just figured it was best to leave him be."

"You didn't ask Mr. Winchester to come?" Claire then asked. "He would have loved an invite. You know how much he likes hanging out with us."

The thought of inviting Mr. Winchester hadn't even crossed Peter's mind. Since he didn't want to admit that fact, he quickly came up with a silly excuse. "Well," he said, "I did think about it. But considering how cold it is, and how old he is, I thought it would be better to just go visit him at his house after their challenge is done."

"You're right, that's probably better," Nicola said. "But someone needs to let him know we're coming over, right?"

* * *

They pulled into the main Meeks parking lot at 8:52, eight minutes before the arranged meeting time. They couldn't spot Zoltan or any of his three trainees, so they randomly picked a picnic table in the sunshine and sat down.

"Should've brought some coffee and cookies," Neil said.

"Coffee?" Peter asked. "Don't tell me you are drinking that junk already?"

"I sure am!" Neil replied. "Well, as long as it's got three creams and at least four packs of sugar in it."

"That's not coffee," Claire laughed. "That's *sugar cream.*"

* * *

Peter checked his watch. 9:04.

"Oh Pete, always obsessed with punctuality," Nicola said, lightly punching him in the arm. "Who cares if they're a little late?"

"Tell you what," Peter said, half-ignoring Nicola's comment. "Since we usually meet up at the picnic tables closer to the river, I'm going to walk over there and take a look. For all we know, they're already sitting over there waiting for us."

"I doubt it," Nicola commented. "But I can see from the expression on your face that you've already made up your mind."

"I'm comin' with you, Petey," Neil announced, standing up quickly. "For moral support."

They all laughed as Peter and Neil started

walking away. Peter, of course, was not in need of any moral support. Neil just wanted to talk to him away from Claire, as he needed some advice about what to buy her for Christmas this year.

"What are you getting Nik?" Neil asked bluntly. "Jewelry or something?"

"I haven't decided yet," Peter replied. "And you know Nik, she's not exactly a materialistic person."

"Ah..." Neil answered. "Whatever that means... hey, do you think you could, like, ask Nik to casually inquire about what Claire wants, and then report back to you? And then you tell me?"

"Sure," Peter replied. "Nik would be cool with that."

"Awesome," Neil said, giving Peter a high-five. "Thanks."

They were now only a few meters away from the picnic tables by the river. No one was at the tables, or anywhere else in sight.

"This is a little weird," Peter said, looking at his watch again. "It's almost a quarter past nine now. They should be here."

"Hey, what's that?" Neil said, pointing at something on one of the picnic tables.

As they got closer, they saw that the "white thing" was an envelope, which was taped to a picnic table. On the front of the envelope, one word was written:

Peter

"Must be a note to say they couldn't show up for some reason," Neil remarked. "Let's take a look."

Peter picked up the envelope and removed the note. As he was taking out the note, something else fell out of the envelope: a key. Attached to the keyring was also a small plate with a number on it.

Neil wasn't looking at the note or the key, but instead at Peter. The color slowly drained completely from Peter's face as he read the long note.

"What's going on?" Neil asked.

Peter couldn't speak. He sat down on the picnic table bench and handed the note to Neil. When Neil saw the first couple of lines of the note, he understood exactly why Peter was terrified.

CHAPTER 18

Greetings Peter! Or perhaps we should refer to you as the naive, stupid, easy to fool Peter! We (Maximilian, Aurora, Cynthia) really only came to Earth with one goal in mind: to kidnap Zoltan. And that, we have successfully done.

The one who sent us here on this mission also gave us a secondary mission, which was to silence you, your friends, your brother, and Mr. Winchester. And by "silence" we were told to use any means necessary. But none of us are killers. (Or at least we don't want to be...) Nor do we have anything personal against any of you.

As you already know, there is nothing weather gods enjoy more than creating or solving a good puzzle, so we have prepared a series of puzzles and challenges for you and your friends. Solving them will give you a chance to find and rescue both Bradley and Mr. Winchester. Oops! I suppose we forgot to mention that we kidnapped them as well... And we've "hidden them away" somewhere. In order to get to them, you'll have to navigate your way through all of the challenges and figure out clues that will take you all over the place.

Good Luck! (We don't really mean that, as we could care less if you find them or not...)

However, if you cheat (and we'll know if you are cheating because we have installed video cameras at all of the locations of the puzzles) then we will "permanently silence" your brother and the old man, if you know what we mean...

This envelope contains the key to a room at the big, new Stoneburg Royal Hotel. We've hung the "Do Not Disturb" sign on the doorknob, so the cleaners will not have been in the room.

Go there, and you'll find the instructions for the first of your challenges.

And don't forget, we'll be watching! The whole time!

Maximilian, Aurora, Cynthia

With a somewhat blank look on his face, Peter sat down, took a few deep breaths, and prepared to collect his thoughts. The psychologist he'd been seeing for a few years, Dr. Stanley, had spent countless sessions helping Peter build an array of simple and effective techniques to use whenever he felt an "emotional volcano" coming on.

Neil had known Peter for a very long time, and vividly remembered how often Peter used to panic, run away, or cry whenever something overwhelmed him. But the changes in Peter over the last three or four years were astounding. Neil was so happy that his best friend was now quite capable of not letting his emotions affect his behavior.

But Neil did feel a little awkward by the silence, so he chose to say something simple, supportive, and true. "Pete," he told his friend. "This wasn't your fault. Don't even entertain the thought that you did something wrong."

"Thanks, man," Peter replied while looking up

at Neil.

Neil casually walked a few steps away from Peter, as he was a little confused about what he should or shouldn't do next.

But Peter knew exactly what to do: He needed to, right here and now, utilize one of the techniques Dr. Stanley had taught him to make sure he stayed in charge of his emotions.

"Okay, Pete," he said softly to himself. "You know what to do: State the facts, man. Say them out loud and believe them." He paused and took a few more deep breaths. "One: As Neil just pointed out, this is NOT your fault. Two: Mr. Winchester and Brad have been kidnapped. Kidnapped. Not hurt or killed or anything like that. Three: There is a way to save them. Four: The way to save them is to solve puzzles, and you are the master of doing that." He paused again and looked over at Neil. "Neil, take the note over to Nik and Claire. I'll catch up with you in a minute."

"Roger," Neil replied, happy to see that Peter was running the show again.

"Okay, Pete," Peter said to himself at a normal volume now that Neil was far enough away that he wouldn't hear anything. "You know what's next: Decide and act."

Before he had even realized it, Peter was pacing in circles. He wasn't doing this because he was worried or nervous, but because it helped him think more clearly.

"The *decide* part is easy," he said to himself. "I mean, there really isn't even an option, is there? Obviously, we take on the challenges."

Peter started walking back, knowing exactly what the *act* part was going to be. "You are going to lead this team," he told himself with fire in his voice. "And the best way to do that is to instill confidence in them the instant you see them. You tell them there's nothing to worry about, and you say it with confidence. Confidence, Pete. *Contagious* confidence."

Peter smiled and started jogging instead of walking. "Thanks, Dr. Stanley," he said, doing the thumbs-up sign with both hands.

As soon as he rounded the corner and his friends were in view, the two girls' body language made it clear that they had had time to read the note.

Nicola ran up and hugged Peter. "I'm sorry, Pete. I'm so sorry," she said, voice a little shaky.

Peter hugged her back. Just because he wanted to be a confident leader didn't mean he wasn't allowed to be compassionate toward his girlfriend.

"Guys," Peter announced after Nicola had gone from hugging to standing beside him with her arm around his waist. "Let's go do what we do best. My brother and our mentor are counting on us. And I am NOT planning on letting them down."

CHAPTER 19

They quickly jogged back to Neil's car and hopped in. Peter was holding the note tightly in one hand and the room key in the other.

"You know how to get there, right?" Claire asked Neil.

"Not exactly," Neil replied. "But isn't this new hotel, like, one of the tallest buildings in Stoneburg? It's somewhere near the city center, right? It shouldn't be that hard to find."

Although all four wanted to get to the hotel as quickly as possible, Neil made sure to obey every single traffic law while driving there, even going as far as keeping his speed a few kilometers under the posted speed limit. (Their parents would always speed, especially on the big highway between Clearville and Stoneburg.) But the last thing a sixteen-year-old new driver needed was a speeding ticket.

* * *

"There it is!" Nicola said, pointing at the tall,

shiny and very modern hotel. "Just keep heading down this road. It should take us right there."

A few minutes later, Neil pulled into the hotel parking garage. "Do you guys want to run in first while I find a place to park?"

Nicola and Claire both turned to face Peter. They clearly wanted him to be in charge of making that decision.

"No," he replied quite quickly. "We are all going in together. We have absolutely no idea what's waiting for us, or what could happen if we split up."

The first available parking spot was on the third floor. Once parked, they all got out and ran to the closest stairwell they could find, and quickly went down to the ground level. Then they walked up to the front entrance of the hotel, and took a few seconds to marvel at the massive revolving door that would let them in.

Peter looked at the key in his hand. It had the number 1124 on the attached tag. They certainly weren't going to be using the stairs to get up there.

This fancy hotel actually had four elevators, so they barely even had to wait after pushing the *up* button. They got in and Peter quickly pushed the *11* and then the *door close* button. When the doors didn't close right away—which is a standard safety feature in all elevators—he started pushing it over and over. (Even though Dr.

Stanley had helped Peter in many ways, the impatient part of Peter's personality still took over occasionally.)

When they finally reached the eleventh floor, he began banging on the *door open* button over and over. "What's taking so long?" he said in frustration. Before his three friends had a chance to tell him to chill out, the doors started to open. Peter jumped out and the rest quickly followed him.

The wall right in front of them had a plate on it, which showed that rooms 1101–1120 were to the left, and 1121–1140 were to the right. Peter took big strides to get to 1124 as quickly as he could.

Nicola, Neil, and Claire jogged to catch up to Peter as he put the key in the lock and twisted it. He pushed the door open and went inside. He was so eager to see what was inside the room that he accidentally forgot to hold the door for Nicola, who was right behind him.

The lights in the room were all on, and just as promised, a single envelope lay on the small table between the two double beds.

"Look, there's the camera they mentioned," Nicola said, pointing at what looked like the kind of security camera you would see in a jewelry shop or convenience store. It was on top of the TV, with the lens facing toward the bedside table. The little red light was on, indicating the camera was indeed working. And since it was wireless, that meant it was somehow hooked up remotely to the location where Maximilian, Aurora, and Cynthia were watching them from.

Claire lightly touched the side of the camera. It didn't slide or twist. "Look," she said. "I think they used double-sided tape or something to stick it to the top of the TV."

"Best we just leave it as is," Nicola advised her. "Tampering with it in any way might make them think we are trying to cheat. And we don't want that."

They sat down on the beds and Peter frantically removed the note from its envelope. He took a deep breath, closed his eyes, and then let the air out. He began reading aloud.

CHAPTER 20

Welcome!

Just in case you are wondering if we are really watching you, the answer is a resounding YES! We can see you and your friends clearly. We've installed cameras like this one at all of the locations for today's wild goose chase. (We found that term in a dictionary, and it seemed quite appropriate...)

Well, enough small talk. (We found that one in a dictionary, too.)

Your first task: Find the next key.

Your instructions: Go up four floors, and then decipher this rhyming clue to locate the key.

*Clue: Your search for a key, so easy to
hide,
We've made not too difficult, as time's
not on your side.
And speaking of time, all people here
certainly save a bit,
By using this, something so simple, but
obviously a big hit!*

"A rhyming hint?" Claire said while shaking her head. "That's a first."

"I'm brutal at these things," Neil said. "I always get Ds in poetry."

"The fact that it rhymes," Peter advised, "means nothing. Zero. This clue is no different than any other clue."

"Ah," Neil nodded. "Okay, thanks Pete."

"Why don't we go up there before we start thinking too hard," Nicola suggested. "It might be easier to decipher once we're up there."

"Good call, Nik," Peter replied. He folded the note in half and slid it into his back pocket, and picked up the 1124 room key and put it in his backpack. His sixth sense told him he just might have to get back into this room again sometime today; And just like every other decision Peter faced, "better safe than sorry" always played a huge role...

They left room 1124 and went back to the elevators. It didn't take long before one arrived, and when it opened, thankfully no one else was inside. They all hopped in, Peter leading the way, and he immediately pushed the *15*. Then just like he had done last time, he started rapidly pushing the *door close* button again.

When they got up to the fifteenth floor, they exited the elevator in a rush. But after that, no one really knew what to do next. Before Nicola, Neil or Claire had a chance to ask Peter if he had any idea where to start looking, Peter had taken the note out of his pocket, and was reading it aloud again.

"How about this," Nicola suggested as soon as Peter finished the rhyme. "What if we, I don't know, start walking around or something? Maybe we'll see something that helps?"

"Sounds good to me, Nik," Neil said. "How about Claire and I check the hallway on the right, and you and Pete do the same on the left? The hallways aren't that long, so if anyone sees something, just shout and the other two can run over."

"Awesome plan, Neil," Peter said. "Let's do it."

Peter and Nicola walked to the left hallway, which was for rooms 1501–1520. The hallway was quite fancy, as least as far as hotels go. The carpet looked very expensive, and paintings lined the walls on both sides. And there were large, elaborate vases at both ends of the hallway.

"I bet the riddle has to do with something in

one of the paintings," Nicola said.

"I was thinking the same thing," Peter replied. "I'm pretty sure that the rhyme is telling us to look for something... uh... simple or convenient. Let's look through each painting and see which one or ones show convenient items or things like that."

"Sounds good, Pete," Nicola replied. "I'll do this side and you do that one."

"Neil! Claire!" Nicola shouted. "We think the answer is going to be hidden in one of the paintings!"

"Uh... okay," Neil *kind of* replied. "But what are we looking for?"

"Something convenient!" she said back loudly. "You know, like something that would, I don't know, save you time!"

"Gotcha," Neil answered.

As Peter moved from painting to painting, there seemed to be no rhyme or reason to them. Some were of animals, some of old homes, some of nature, and some were just abstract obscurities.

* * *

"Anything Nik?" Peter asked after checking the last painting on his side, the one just beside room 1520.

"Not yet," she replied. She had been spending more time than Peter on each one, so there were still four or five on her side that she hadn't looked at.

"Okay," Peter said, a little impatiently. "I'll help look at the last few on your side."

* * *

Neil and Claire had adopted a slightly different approach for their scanning of the paintings. They stayed together while looking at each one: Claire stood very close and Neil stood a few steps back.

On their sixth painting, Claire spotted something promising. "Neil, come closer," she said. "Look at this." She was pointing at the shirt pocket on one of the men in the painting. More specifically, at the mechanical pencil in that man's shirt pocket.

"A mechanical pencil," Neil said. "Those things certainly are convenient. And they save time, right? No more using pencil sharpeners! And when they were first invented, I bet they were a big hit. I mean, like, EVERYONE uses them now!"

"Pete! Nik!" Claire shouted. "Come over here. We've found something!"

Peter and Nicola ran as fast as they could to get there. Upon closer inspection, they both agreed that Claire had found what might be the right painting.

"So if this is the right one," Claire asked. "Then where would the key be?"

"Not sure," Peter answered. "But in all likelihood, it's probably taped to the top of the frame. Or maybe on the back. Those would be the only places where it would be completely out of sight."

Neil jumped high to get a look at the top of the frame. "Not on the top," he said.

Claire then carefully pulled the bottom part of the painting away from the wall by about twenty centimeters. Peter stuck his face in behind it to look for the key.

"Guys," he said with obvious disappointment in his voice, "it's not here."

"Are you sure?" Neil asked, joining Peter behind the painting.

Convinced that they were looking at the wrong painting, Claire slowly lowered it back to its original position.

"There are still a few more to check in this hallway," Claire said. "One of them has got to be hiding that key."

With the four of them working together now, they finished their scans of the remaining paintings in no time. But none of them contained anything that could be considered even remotely convenient.

"Man," Peter said in frustration, after looking at the final painting.

"Hold up, Pete," Neil said. "We haven't looked at the vases yet."

"True," Peter replied. "But vases aren't exactly new, convenient items."

"And they don't save people time, either," Claire added. But she was careful to say it in a way that made it clear she wasn't making fun of Neil's suggestion.

Peter started walking back down the hallway. "Guys, I'm going to sit down on those chairs near the elevators," he said. "I wanna reread the rhyme a few more times. I need to think it through a little more carefully.

They followed their *fearless leader*—who was beginning to appear a little agitated—back to the chairs. Then they listened to the rhyming hint again, three times in total, a little slower each time.

"Why can't we figure this out, guys?" Peter said after the third reading. "The answer is probably staring us right in the face."

Claire's eyes lit up. Really, really lit up.

"What is it?" Neil said to her. "You've got an idea, don't you?"

Claire, smiling, pointed at the sign on the wall. The one right above Peter's head, that showed which rooms were to the left and which were to the right.

"That sign," Claire explained, "is certainly convenient. It tells guests whether to go left or right after they get off the elevator."

Peter jumped up from his seat to look at the sign. He could barely contain his excitement. "Which saves time," Peter said, "for EVERYONE who stays here! Claire, you're brilliant!"

Peter felt around the frame of the sign to see where the key might be taped. Unlike the painting, this sign wasn't hanging from the wall, it was screwed to it. So the only place the key could be hidden was somewhere on the frame.

He slid his fingers along all four sides. On the top, he collected a lot of dust on his finger while doing so. (The cleaning staff at this hotel was obviously not as meticulous as his mother when it came to dusting...)

"It's not here," he said, sounding both surprised and upset.

"Don't give up so quickly," Neil said supportively. "They probably couldn't tape it to the sign. It would have been too obvious to the hotel staff. It's probably hidden under one of the chairs here. Or maybe under this little table."

A very close inspection of the table and chairs revealed their worst fears: no key.

"I bet those three are watching us right now and laughing their heads off," Claire said, looking around to see where the camera had been placed.

"I don't see a camera anywhere," Neil said. "Looks like that *we'll be watching you* threat was just a bunch of balderdash."

"Balder what?" Nicola asked.

"Oh," Neil giggled, "that's a word my mom encourages me to use instead of swearing."

"So what do we do then?" Claire asked loudly.

"I mean, is this actually even a puzzle? Or are they just running us around and taking us for fools?"

Peter was already a few meters away from his team, pacing around in a discombobulated pattern. He wasn't prepared to accept that this could be a trick. Nor was he ready to say that this puzzle was too hard.

But something certainly was amiss. There should be a camera watching them, but there wasn't. And the key should be taped to the sign directing people to their rooms, but it wasn't.

Peter did what he often did when stuck, he took the note out again and began rereading it ad nauseum to himself. Nicola, Neil, and Claire remained silent, knowing this was not the time to disturb him.

This carried on for quite some time. Claire, who was the least familiar with Peter's quirky habits, eventually broke the silence. A little louder than she should have, she said, "Maybe today just isn't our lucky day."

Neil tried to shush her, but it was too late. Peter hated (actually despised) and completely disagreed with the concept of luck. He had caught Claire's comment. He stopped pacing and glared at her.

"Sorry, Pete," she said softly. "I was, just, like, uh…"

Peter looked at the note again. His face began

to change. It wasn't one of frustration, but one of amazement. "Claire, thank you!" he said loudly. Then he crushed the note into a ball and hit the elevator button.

"Are we going back to 1124?" Neil asked.

"No sir," Peter smiled. "As you can see, I pushed the *up* button, not the *down* one.

"Up? Why?" Claire asked.

"Because, Claire, my dear," Peter replied with a silly smirk. "You just reminded me of something when you said the word *lucky*."

"Really?" she asked.

"I don't get it," Neil added.

The elevator came and they all stepped inside. "Look at the buttons," Peter said. "Notice anything?"

"Uh…" Neil answered. "Nope… why?"

"Okay," Peter continued. "Then follow my fingers."

Peter pointed at the 11, then the 12, and then… the next button was the 14.

"Wait! I get it!" Claire yelled. "Hotels don't have a thirteenth floor! People think it's unlucky!"

"Nicely done," Peter said.

"So that means," Nicola added, "that we actually only went up three floors, not four like the note instructed."

"You got it!" Peter replied.

Claire hit the *16* and they all waited. Time

seemed to slow to a snail's pace before the elevator took off.

When they stepped off on the 16th floor, Neil looked around in search of the camera. He spotted it, concealed very well, in the corner above one of the elevator entrances. Just like the one that had been taped on top of the TV in room 1124, this one also had a red light on.

Peter strode over to the room direction sign and felt around it with his fingers. As he slid them across the top, he felt something, which he knew without looking was the key. It had been taped to the top, in a way that no one could ever have seen unless they had been looking for it.

"Awesome job!" Nicola said loudly, giving him a big hug.

Peter hugged her back, and then walked over to Claire and gave her a powerful high-five. "Without you," he said to her, "we would never have figured this one out."

Once they'd done enough celebrating, Peter looked more closely at the key. It was a key to a home. It looked like one for a doorknob, or possibly a deadbolt. On one side the key, a very small piece of paper had been glued. The paper only had two words on it, which were written in very tiny letters:

Winchester's house

So now they knew where this wild goose chase was going to take them next.

CHAPTER 21

Once they were back in Neil's car and "ready to roll," a strange silence seemed to fall over everyone.

It was Nicola who decided to speak up first. "This is getting really weird, guys," she said. "First, starting us off at a hotel in Stoneburg? And now sending us to Mr. Winchester's?"

"I'd call it mega-super weird," Neil added. "Why didn't he just set up the next challenge in the hotel room?"

"Unfortunately," Peter interjected, not meaning to be rude. "We have to try our best not to think about those things. All we can do is solve the puzzles and follow where the clues lead us. If we do that, eventually we WILL get to Mr. Winchester and Brad."

"Okay," Neil replied. "I'll do what I can to keep the *Neilster* part of my brain focused."

"Anyone hungry or thirsty?" Peter asked while reaching into his backpack. "I brought a couple boxes of granola bars, and, like, nine juice boxes. I was planning on us having these at a picnic table back at Meek's Park while *they* did *our* puzzle."

"Sure," Neil said, happy that the conversation was on the topic of food. "What have you got?"

"Let's see," Peter replied, looking at the two boxes. "Chocolate chip... or honey and oats."

"Score me one of each, if you don't mind," Neil said. "I skipped breakfast... And what are my juice choices?"

"This isn't a restaurant," Claire jokingly scolded him.

"Certainly isn't," Nicola followed. "Because Peter would make the worst waiter ever."

"What are you talking about?" Peter laughed. "I'd be a great waiter!"

"No, you wouldn't," she said back. "You'd get too nervous. You'd fumble your words and leave all the customers super confused."

"Settle down, boys and girls," Neil joked. "Let's get back to what's important here... what drinks have you got?"

"Apple, orange, or mixed fruit," Peter replied. "The apple and orange are one hundred percent fruit juice, but the mixed fruit one has added sugar. So even though it may taste better, it—"

"See!" Nicola jumped in. "What kind of waiter would launch into that explanation when—"

"Mixed fruit!" Neil announced. "I need the extra sugar to help me concentrate."

Peter took a mixed fruit box, removed the little plastic drinking straw attached to its side, and stuck it through the hole.

"I'll hold it for you," he said to Neil. "And just let me know every time you wanna take a sip."

"You guys are so weird," Claire said.

"Thanks, baby!" Neil replied sarcastically, winking so she could see it in the rear-view mirror.

CHAPTER 22

When they got to Mr. Winchester's home, Peter suggested that they be very cautious before approaching the front door. He had a feeling that this would be an easy place for Maximilian, Aurora, and Cynthia to have set up some kind of trap. And if they had, he didn't plan on falling for it.

"Better safe than sorry, right?" he said as they got out of the car.

"You're the boss," Neil replied.

Before getting anywhere near the front door, they walked around the entire house once, making sure to keep a reasonable distance between them and the house the whole time. Nothing looked suspicious or out of place.

Confident that there weren't any traps, they began to walk up the sidewalk and then the front steps. When they were safely up on the front porch, Peter walked to the front door and put the key in the deadbolt. He nervously twisted the key and then took the cold doorknob in his right hand and turned it.

After pushing the heavy door open, he saw a single white envelope on the floor, just beyond the inside floor mat. He knelt down and picked it up.

"Pete, you okay?" Nicola asked.

"Yeah," he answered hesitantly. "But I'm really worried about Mr. Winchester. I mean he's not exactly in perfect health, and if they've duct-taped him to a chair, and—"

"Oh, Pete," Neil said, slapping him on the shoulder. "You're letting that crazy imagination of yours run wild again. Think about it: they aren't from Earth. There's no way they'd ever even consider doing something like that."

"He's right," Claire said. "You've gotta get that mind of yours out of worry mode."

"Easier said than done," Peter whispered to himself. His mind spent more time in worry mode than it did in any other mode.

Neil took the envelope from Peter and removed the note. He read it aloud slowly and clearly.

> *Such a big and lovely house for an old and clever man! So many possible places for us to hide your next clue! But we didn't make this one too hard either.*
>
> *Here's your hint:*

knobs
levers
switches

What are you waiting for? Don't just stand there! Get running!

"Dudes," Neil said. "That trio would get an *F* in poetry."

"No kidding," Peter added. "It's like they wanted to make a rhyming clue again, but then when they couldn't, they just wrote down three words."

"Let's go sit down together at the kitchen table," Nicola suggested. "I'm willing to bet that there is a hidden clue within those three words.

"I like your thinking, Nik," Claire said. "That's better than just running around the house senselessly."

Since Claire knew where Mr. Winchester kept his papers and pencils, she got enough for everyone.

"Now I'm not saying this is the right thing to do," Nicola said with slightly less confidence than a minute ago, "but here's my, uh… advice: write those three words down somewhere on your paper. Then just keep looking at them. Look for… I don't know… for… I don't want to say too much, 'cause if I do, then we'll all end up looking for the same thing."

"Uh... okay," Peter replied. "And how about we do this in silence?"

"Sure, cool," Neil replied.

"Alright," Peter said. "Let's see what we can come up with in five minutes, starting now."

Peter pressed the start button on his wristwatch.

The silence was very awkward at first, but in no time at all, all four were immersed in their own thoughts. Not knowing what the others were thinking of made it that much more intriguing to Peter.

When Peter looked down at his watch and saw that about three minutes had passed, he couldn't help but take a peek at Nicola's and Claire's papers. He immediately realized they were doing more or less the same thing; they were trying to rearrange the letters to spell other words. Peter had a feeling they were on the right track. But just in case they weren't, he wanted to take his own mind down a different one. The more options the better, right?

"Time's up," Peter announced the instant the timer on his watch hit five minutes. "So what d'ya got?"

"Actually, I got a little overwhelmed there," Nicola said. "I mean, considering the number of letters, there are just way too many words that can be spelled." She showed them her list:

shelves
rest
is
it
with
vest
see
his
know
best
hiss
bee
rose

"Hey, my list looks pretty similar to yours," Claire said. "We have lots of the same words written down. But how do we know which ones actually mean something?"

"Well, the nouns on your list at least give us somewhere to start," Peter explained. "You know, like shelves. We can go to his bookshelves and look there."

"I don't mean to tell you that you're barking up the wrong tree," Neil said apprehensively, "but I looked at this puzzle completely differently. I tried to think of a place in a house that has knobs, levers, and switches. And I think the clue is telling us to go to a washroom. More specifically, the ensuite one that has a shower in it."

"A washroom?" Claire asked. "Why?"

"Well, uh…" Neil said. "There are knobs on all the cabinets, levers for the sink and shower, and the main fuse box—you know, that big yellow thing that controls the electricity for the whole house—is mounted above the door in the ensuite bathroom. And that sucker is loaded with switches."

"Can't do us any harm to check it out," Peter agreed.

They all went through the master bedroom into the ensuite bathroom and started looking around for the next clue. They checked everywhere they could think of: under the mat, in each and every drawer, and in the medicine cabinet. They even took off the top of the toilet tank and looked in there.

"Guys!" Neil said suddenly. "Check it out! I found it!"

Mr. Winchester's bathroom had been renovated a year and a half ago. They had removed the big old bathtub and replaced it with a shower unit. He had the contractors install bars along the walls both inside and outside the shower, to reduce his chance of having a bad fall. They had also bolted a sturdy plastic seat in the shower which was set in a fairly high position. That way he could sit down while showering and stand up quite easily when finished.

Neil opened the clear glass door of the shower stall and pointed at the message that had been written in blue crayon on the light beige shower seat.

Just as he got ready to read what it said, he looked up and spotted the camera, which was taped to the ceiling and pointing straight down at his face. They had definitely found the right room.

Well done! You are quite a team! Peter, you must be running things very well. Or, is someone else running this group? Or is no one running anything?

"Guys," Neil said, baffled by the meaning of the new clue. "This doesn't make any sense at all."

"Certainly doesn't," Claire added. "The messages keep getting more and more cryptic."

"Something's not right," Peter said. "I have no idea what, but something just isn't right."

"Pete," Nicola said. "Pass me the note."

She read it quietly to herself while the other three waited for her to say something.

Peter, impatient to hear what was going on in her mind, couldn't help but ask, "What is it Nik? You got—"

"Shh…" Claire said, covering Peter's mouth with her hand. "Give her some time. Just like you, she probably thinks more clearly when left undisturbed."

"Sorry," Peter whispered to Claire.

But being silent didn't mean the same as doing nothing. For his entire life, Peter had clearly been unable to "sit still."

* * *

When Peter was in Grade 3, his teacher had pointed out Peter's "excessive restlessness" to his parents, and recommended they consult a specialist.

Peter, although only eight at the time, still remembers being told he may have a mild form of ADHD. He also recalls how the specialist thought that he shouldn't be in the room while she explained to his parents exactly what ADHD was. So during that fifteen-minute span, he sat in the waiting room, sucking on a lollipop the receptionist had given him. On the drive home, his parents seemed no different than usual, so Peter figured that was a good sign.

But once home, curiosity got the better of him and he asked his mom if she could take him to the library the next morning, which was a Saturday. He said he wanted to borrow some books on the solar system, since they had just started learning the basics of it in science, and he thought it was really cool. Peter's "second" favorite place in the world was the library. (His "first" was the games/hobby shop at the mall.) And he never needed any help finding the books he was looking for, as he had long since mastered the library's shelving system.

So that Saturday, while his mom flipped through sewing magazines and sipped coffee, Peter found a book on ADHD and read through a couple of chapters while sitting on a step stool between aisles. He chose that odd location to read so his mom wouldn't know where he was.

Having read enough, he put the book back and went quickly to the science section. He grabbed the first two solar system books he saw. Then he went to his mom and said, "Thanks mom, I found two good ones."

"And don't you forget, young man," his mom responded, "that you promised to polish the silverware if I brought you here today." Peter's mom never ever forgot anything...

* * *

So Peter just attributed his overactive mind and body to ADHD. He walked out of the washroom and went back to the living room, where he paced around in a loop thinking and rethinking the message Neil had just read.

"Pete!" Neil yelled. "Get back here! Nik's got something!"

"Yessss!" Peter said, pumping his fist. He knew Nicola was great at cracking these kinds of codes.

"Okay, here's what I'm thinking," she said once Peter was back in the washroom. "The word *running* was used in the first note, and then again three more times in the message on the shower seat. That can't be a coincidence."

"You wouldn't think so," Claire said.

"So, *we* certainly can't be running in here," Nicola said. "But... the water can."

"The water?" Peter asked.

"Yeah," she went on. "Let's turn on the hot water for the sink and the shower and—"

"Why?" Peter said, interrupting her.

"Pete," Nicola said softly, taking his hand, "C'mon, just trust me here."

Peter always wanted to know the answers to all the *whys* before acting, but apparently was not going to have that luxury this time. He managed to hold his questions back, and cranked on the hot water for both the sink and shower.

Nothing happened at first, but as steam built up in the bathroom, they could see a message had been written for them on the mirror above the sink, and a second one on the inside of the shower door. And these only became visible because the surfaces were now covered in condensation.

Above the sink, were three words:

Go back to

And on the inside of the shower was a number:

1124

"Awesome, Nik," Peter exclaimed, hugging her.

"Those three are pretty good at making tough puzzles, eh?" Neil said.

"Well, somewhat true," Peter answered. "But they haven't been able to fool us yet!"

"Pete, you've still got the key, right?" Neil asked as they ran out of Mr. Winchester's house and back to his car.

"Think about who you are talking to," Peter answered his friend with a smile. "You know I'm *mister overly prepared and excessively paranoid.* Of course I kept it! It's in my backpack! But now that you've said that, let me double-check..."

CHAPTER 23

Neil took the exact same route they had used to drive to Mr. Winchester's house to get them back to the big hotel in Stoneburg. And once again, he made absolutely sure not to break any traffic laws. (Even though everyone else on the highway kept whizzing past them.)

Once they had parked, entered the hotel, and were in the elevator heading up to floor eleven, Claire commented on something which Peter had actually been pondering himself.

"If they're sending us back here again," she said, "that means they must be fairly close by."

"I bet they are in this hotel somewhere," Neil said. "I mean, we know Zoltan was provided with a huge amount of money, right? If they've trapped him, and taken it all, they certainly could have booked more than one room. Wait... maybe they are even holding Mr. Winchester and Brad here, too!?"

"The tough thing," Peter said, "is figuring out

which room they're in."

"First things first, everyone," Nicola said as the elevator doors opened and they started their walk back to 1124. "Let's see what they've left for us. We can think about *playing detective* later."

"Peter unlocked the door and they all went back inside the room they had been in only a couple of hours ago. Only one thing was different. And it wasn't only different, but it was also obviously part of the next puzzle.

On the table between the two beds, where the phone and alarm clock had previously been, there were now four digital timers. They were quite small, maybe half the size of an alarm clock. They were lined up neatly in a row. They reminded Peter of the timers that were used at the finish line of the 100-meter dash to display the winner's time. Each timer was set to a different time, and none of them were counting either up or down. The four timers, in order, were set to:

2:06   6:18   46:14   30:45

They looked around the room for an envelope, but there clearly wasn't one for them this time. So this weird combination of numbers contained the clue about where to go or what to do next.

Neil decided to say each time aloud, if for no other reason than to convey how confused he was. "Two minutes and six seconds, six eighteen, forty-six fourteen, and thirty forty-five," he announced, trying to mimic the voice a sports caster would use when calling names as athletes cross a finish line.

Then Neil did something very out of character. He walked up and put his face right in front of the camera and said, "We don't need to see you to know that you're all laughing like crazy right now!" He paused, took a few steps back, pointed at the timers, and continued, "But I guarantee, unequi..." He paused, as the word he wanted to say had suddenly vanished.

"Unequivocally," Peter said, helping Neil out.

"Unequivocally," Neil continued, "that we will figure this one out. So laugh away now, while you still can!"

As Neil sat back down on one of the beds, Peter turned toward the timers and glared at them, as if it was *Peter vs. the timers* in a gladiator pit. Peter considered himself the king of number puzzles, and Neil's comments to the camera twenty seconds earlier had only made him even more eager to break this code as fast as he could. He closed his eyes for a few seconds and took a couple of deep breaths.

With his eyes still shut, he began to speak, "Guys, I'll try my absolute best to figure this out. But the more help you give me, the better."

Nicola had already taken Peter's hand before he opened his eyes back up, "Pete," she said. "Of course we are going to help you. We would never make you tackle one of these on your own."

"No kidding, dude," Neil laughed. "Don't go all mushy on us!"

Claire laughed at that, followed immediately by Nicola and Peter too. The contagious laughter went on for a good thirty seconds, and all of their faces were red before they settled back down.

All four looked toward the timers again, with their "thinking caps" on now. Peter reached into his backpack and took out pencils and papers for everyone. (He'd "borrowed" a bunch from Mr. Winchester's house, just in case they needed to use them again). Just like they'd done at Mr. Winchester's, they decided to start by thinking separately.

Peter tried his best to keep his eyes off their papers, but couldn't resist a quick peek at Neil's.

Neil was calculating the time difference between each of the timers. He had written those three numbers down, but the baffled expression on Neil's face indicated he had no clue what to do with them next.

Since he'd already looked at Neil's paper—and considering his own was completely blank—Peter decided to walk over to the small circular table in the corner where Nicola and Claire were sitting and working together at it.

As Peter approached, Claire told him what they were up to. "Nik and I," Claire said, "are both thinking the same thing. We think each number represents a letter. So if we can figure out which letter corresponds to each number, we should be able to spell out the answer."

"Ahh... I see," Peter replied. "That's good thinking."

"We haven't produced any words yet, but here's what we are on to," Claire explained. "Notice how each timer has either a zero or a one, and that those are always one of the middle digits of each timer. Never the first or the last number. That must mean that these are both vowels. Since 'u' is the least used vowel, that means we only have four others to choose from. So we are currently experimenting with different combinations."

"If we can figure out the third timer," Nicola added, "which has a *4* at both the start and the end, then we should be able to get the rest of them."

"Neil," Peter said. "Come and give us a hand. Claire and Nik have figured out what to do. If all of us work on it, we'll surely decipher it a lot quicker.

"Well, let's brainstorm ideas for what words forty-six fourteen can spell," Nicola suggested. "And just say anything you come up with."

Everyone started playing around with letters in their mind and on paper, to see what words they could create.

Neil was the first to say something. "I've got

two," he said, "but they're both pretty weird. B-L-O-B, blob. And P-R-O-P, prop."

"Awesome," Nicola said, not wanting to say what she was actually thinking: *only tell us words that could be useful!*

"How about P-R-E-P?" Claire suggested. "Prep is short for preparation, right?"

"The only one I've come up with," Peter said, "is way too morbid. D-I-E-D. Hope it's not that..."

"Could it be that?" Nicola said.

"No way," Peter replied.

"Not died, that, T-H-A-T!" she exclaimed.

"T-H-A-T, eh?" Neil said. "Definitely a common word."

"And it fits nicely into the middle of a short phrase," Nicola added.

"Okay, so let's assume we are right," Peter said. "Then the second word starts with H-A."

"H-A-Y is a word, isn't it?" Neil asked. "You know, hay, the stuff horses eat."

"I can think of quite a few others," Claire added. "There's *had*, *has*, um... and *ham*."

"I think you're onto something," Peter said. "I doubt it's *ham*, though. It's gotta be either *has* or *had*."

"So the clue would be," Nicola said. "*Something* has that *something*. Or *something* had that *something*."

"And since *had* is just the past tense of *has*," Claire said right away, "then it shouldn't really matter which one we use."

"Plus, we already know the number *4*, which is the third letter in the last word, is a *T*," Peter added.

"Cool," Neil said. "Let's see what we can come up with for the fourth word."

There was a minute or two where no one spoke as they mentally ran through the alphabet, trying to find words that both worked and made sense.

Neil broke the silence. "*Has that fits?*" he said awkwardly.

"*Has that duty*," Nicola said right after him.

"Both usable," Peter nodded. "Any others?"

"I've got two, actually," Claire said excitedly. "*Has that cuts*. Or *has that bite*."

"Those are good, too," Peter said happily. "But figuring out which one is correct is going to be tough."

"Yeah," Neil followed. "Like, all four of those phrases point at totally different things."

"Then maybe," Peter suggested, "we need to crack word one first."

"Sounds good, Pete," Claire agreed. "Let's give it a shot."

"Hold on a sec, everyone," Neil said suddenly, but in a tone that sounded not at all promising or positive. "I think we are, and pardon me for using this cheesy expression again, barking up the wrong tree."

"What do you mean?" Peter asked.

"Well, the *6* is an *H*, right?" Neil explained. "So the first word ends in an *H?* I don't know any words, or at least any three-letter English words, that end in an *H...*"

"You're right," Nicola said.

"Aaargh," Claire said loudly. "This is so frustrating!"

"Don't let it get to you," Nicola said while patting Claire on the back. "We've all felt the same way before, overwhelmed by puzzles like this."

"I feel like my brain is going to blow up!" Claire blurted out.

"Tell you what everyone," Peter suggested. "Let's take five. Do whatever you want for five or ten minutes, but DO NOT think about this puzzle. You'd be amazed how big a difference a little breather can make."

Claire and Nicola leaned back in their chairs, and Peter went and sat on the edge of one of the beds. Unable to just sit there and do nothing, he picked up the remote. He knew he needed some alternate stimulation to truly get his mind out of the puzzle.

While Peter started channel surfing, Neil lay down on his back across one of the beds. Since Peter had ended up choosing a news channel which was talking about some money laundering scandal—something that Neil had zero interest in listening to—Neil turned his head away from the TV. Of course, this meant he was now looking right at the four timers again. His head was hanging off the edge of the bed a little, so it was almost as if he was looking at them upside down.

"You guys aren't going to believe this until you see it!" Neil announced loudly and proudly.

Peter hit the mute button on the TV, and Nicola and Claire stood up and came closer.

Neil was sitting up on the bed now, waiting for his audience.

Neil picked the timers up, turned them upside down, and then placed the upside-down timers back in their original spots on the table.

"Man," he said loudly. "What a group of tricksters!"

He got no reaction, at all, from his team.

"Oh, please," he said with a huge grin. "Someone tell me you can see it too."

Still silence.

"Okay, but this will make it way too obvious," Neil continued. "You must remember when we were in, like, Grade 4 or so, and we would enter numbers in a calculator, flip it upside down, and show everyone whatever rude or inappropriate words the upside-down numbers looked like?"

"Neil!" Peter said, giving him a huge high-five. "You're a genius, man!"

"The second, third and fourth ones are easy, BIG HIGH SHOE," Nicola said. "But the first one doesn't make any sense. What is G-O-Z? I've never heard of the word goz."

"It's not goz," Neil explained. "The 2 is to, you know T-O. So the first timer says: *GO TO.*"

"Go to big high shoe?" Claire asked. "What's that supposed to mean?"

"I know exactly what it means," Neil said while standing up and darting for the door. "Let's go, I'll explain in the elevator. No time to waste!"

Unfortunately, there was a family of three in the same elevator, so Neil had to wait until they were outside and heading for the car before he could explain anything.

"They want us to go to that big statue of the soccer ball and soccer shoe," he said.

"I know that one," Claire added. "That really ugly bronze statue behind Livingston Stadium!"

"I do agree it's ugly," Peter said, "but I can't speak badly about it. The funds for building the stadium, along with all the practice grounds around the stadium, were all donated by Alfred Livingston. He had played semi-pro soccer sometime in the past."

"Wait a second," Neil added. "Is that the local guy who won big in the lottery?"

"That's him," Peter answered. "And he thought, for some reason we'll never understand, that putting a statue there would look cool."

"Ah," Nicola said, "and since he was covering the bill, no one could tell him *no.*"

"Exactly," Peter answered.

They were now back at the car. Neil quickly unlocked the doors and they all got in.

"To the statue Mr. Chauffeur!" Peter said in a silly accent.

"With pleasure, sir," Neil replied, copying Peter's ridiculous accent. "But not till you all fasten your seat belts!"

CHAPTER 24

About fifteen minutes later, they arrived at the beautiful Livingston Stadium. Since it was not soccer season, the parking lot was virtually empty. They parked in the corner nearest the statue and quickly jogged over to it.

Before anyone spotted the note, Neil pointed to the camera that had been taped high up on the *ball* part of the big statue. The lens was aiming down, giving whoever was watching a clear view of everyone at or near the statue.

"That camera wouldn't be up there if this was the wrong place," Neil said.

They started scanning every part of the shoe for the note. Claire found it, taped in a crevice under one part of the shoelace. A typical passer-by would never have seen it by accident. (But the statue was so ugly that most people did what they could to avoid it anyway...)

"What's it say?" Neil asked impatiently. "What are we supposed to do?"

"Hold your horses," Peter said to Neil. Right after he said that expression—which he had never heard anyone other than his mother use—he added, "Just give her a second. She hasn't even opened the envelope yet."

Claire hopped down from the statue, pulled out the note, and began reading aloud.

> *Well done! You certainly are better at these puzzles than we expected.*
>
> *So now what?*
>
> *We certainly can't make you do one here in public, can we? So we could think of no better place than Silverhead Mountain for the rest of your challenges.*
>
> *Everything has been set up. Just drive out there, park in the small parking lot where the three hiking trails begin, and follow the map on the back of this note.*

"This really does feel like a wild goose chase, doesn't it?" Neil commented.

"Yeah," Peter gulped. "Unfortunately, we all know whatever's waiting for us at Silverhead Mountain is going to be harder than anything we have done so far. Waaay harder."

"Petey boy," Neil said, puffing his chest up.

"Neil," Claire said, interrupting him. "Don't even think about using that ridiculous nickname for yourself right now. We all know you're about to tell us *we can count on the Neilster*, right?"

Peter and Nicola started laughing, as Claire had just hit the nail on the head.

Ignoring Claire's comment, Neil smirked. "Never underestimate the power of the Neilster," he said in a deep, mysterious tone, as if he were imitating the evil character in a spy movie.

"Okay, fine, *Mr. Neilster*," Claire said in between laughs. "But for now, can't you just... uh, drive?"

"As you command, your highness of all highnesses," he replied in a low voice again, doing an awful rendition of a sinister grin.

CHAPTER 25

They began the drive out to Silverhead Mountain, a location that everyone other than Claire knew all too well. There wasn't too much conversation going on, as everyone's level of fear began to rise as they got closer to their destination.

Since she'd never been there before, Claire was extremely curious as to what to expect. "Can someone tell me why Silverhead Mountain is always the spot that is chosen for the challenges?" she asked.

"It's because of the structures, buildings, and ruins left over from whatever ancient civilization lived there," Peter explained.

"Yeah," Nicola added. "It's like Machu Pichu meets the Pyramids, with some ancient Rome and medieval castles thrown into the mix. It's too bad we are going there to do these challenges, as it's totally fascinating as a sightseeing spot."

"Oh..." Claire replied, in what seemed like a combination of confusion, amazement, and terror.

* * *

After what felt like an eternity, but was actually only a fourteen-minute drive, they pulled into the parking lot. Peter had already examined the map very carefully during the drive, so he was pretty confident they'd be able to follow it successfully. The map was quite detailed and had arrows indicating exactly where they had to trek.

"Am I the only one who's thinking this is some kind of trap?" Claire asked. "I mean, according to Pete, we start by walking down a very narrow path, then turn right where there's a huge boulder to climb over."

"Technically speaking," Peter replied, "anything's possible. And considering who we are dealing with, trust is definitely not a word I would feel comfortable using. But like I said earlier, we really don't have any other choice."

"I guess you're right," Claire said back. "But is it okay if I walk in the middle of the group?"

"Of course, babe," Neil said. "Pete'll lead, Nik behind him, then you, and I'll take up the rear."

"Makes sense," Peter said. "Just don't forget to look behind you every so often. You know, to make sure no one is following us."

Peter wished he hadn't said that, as all it did was make an already scared Claire even more terrified. He quickly followed his comment with one to try to undo the damage. "But I HIGHLY doubt that's going to happen," he told her.

The map was quite simple to follow, but the route it was taking them on was nowhere near easy to traverse. They had to push through huge bushes, scramble over numerous boulders, climb up a couple of fairly steep rock faces, and even walk through a stream at one point. But they were, slowly but surely, approaching what was shown as an arched brick area on the map, labeled "ENTRANCE."

"Look, there it is!" Nicola announced. After over twenty minutes of trekking along a path they would never be able to retrace without the map, they'd arrived at the eerie-looking entrance.

"And look, there's another camera," Neil pointed out. The camera had been attached to the top of the arch, its lens facing outward. A white envelope was wedged tightly in between two of the bricks. No doubt it contained the instructions to the first of the challenges that lay beyond the arch. Peter took the envelope and handed it to Nicola.

"I'm too nervous right now to read it aloud," he said, hands trembling quite a bit. "Would you mind?"

"Of course not," she said as she opened it. Once she'd unfolded the note, she tightly gripped Peter's hand, and then began reading.

CHAPTER 26

Peter, Neil, Nicola, Claire,

After you walk through the entrance and down the tunnel (Don't worry, we have lit the torches on the tunnel walls so you won't be in the dark...) you will come to a room that then branches off into 4 separate tunnels. Above each one of those 4 tunnels, there will be a sign. The sign has the name of the person who is to use that tunnel. All four of you are to enter your respective tunnels at the same time. Once you've reached the end of your individual tunnels, you'll each end up in separate small rooms. Each of those rooms will have four doors, and those doors will be numbered.

There will be a clue, in an envelope on

the floor, waiting for each of you in your rooms. You must figure out, ON YOUR OWN, which of the four doors to open by solving a riddle. And by the way, all four of you will have different riddles.

If you choose the correct door, it will open to a new tunnel. That tunnel will take you to an area where you will reunite with anyone else on your team who also chose the correct door. The other three doors in each room, the incorrect ones, spell doom for you all! (Don't worry, it doesn't trigger a bomb or anything like that...)

If anyone twists the knob of a wrong door, it triggers a mechanism that locks all sixteen doors. And since all of you must get through this challenge for it to be considered complete, that means no one can make even a single mistake!

Nicola looked at her three teammates, wondering who was going to react first. It appeared as if everyone was still in a state of shock.

After a fairly long silence, Claire said, "Guys, this is not good. I mean, you three have done plenty of these kinds of challenges. But I've only done, like, a few."

"That's not true," Nicola said quickly, hoping to quash Claire's fear and negativity. "You haven't faced so many challenges *under these circumstances*, but you have been doing lots of the ones that we have been creating for each other over the past few months."

"She's right," Peter added. "And not only are you really good at puzzles, you are also exceptionally smart. There's no way that trio's riddle will fool you."

Claire's face reddened a little. It was pretty embarrassing to hear how highly they thought of her.

"I had a feeling that one of the challenges was going to be an individual one," Peter continued. "Well, it was probably more like a *fear* than a feeling."

"Anyway, guys," Neil said quite loudly. "Whether all together or all apart, a puzzle is a puzzle."

"That doesn't make much sense," Claire said while giggling.

"Uh... I suppose it doesn't," Neil admitted, giggling a little himself. "But how much of what I say usually does?"

"Well, I've known you a long time," Peter said to Neil. "And I've become pretty good at translating what you say into what you mean. I think what he means is, well, uh..."

"You said you understood him!" Nicola said with a laugh.

Now everyone was laughing. But it didn't sound like genuine "that was funny" laughter. Part of it, or possibly even most of it, could easily be interpreted as nervous laughter.

"Guys," Peter suggested. "Let's sit down for a while before we do this."

Since they were not looking forward to the pressure of what lay ahead, no one objected to Peter's idea. They all sat cross-legged in a circle, so close that their knees were touching.

"I won't pretend I am the superstar coach who is going to give you a pep talk about how to hit the game-winning shot," he began. "All I want to say is this: Take. Your. Time… Read the riddle. Reread it. And then reread it again and again. There's no need to rush. Take as long as you need. And DON'T put your hand on a doorknob until you are a hundred and ten percent sure it's the correct one."

"Got it," Neil replied, somewhat unaware that he really didn't need to reply. Claire and Nicola also nodded, indicating they had caught the gist of what Peter had just said.

Peter stood up. "Okay, team," he said. "Let's do this."

Peter first, followed by Claire and Nicola (who were holding hands because they were so scared) and then finally Neil entered the long tunnel. It twisted and weaved a few times. And in a couple of spots, parts of the walls and ceiling had crumbled off, so they had to walk very cautiously.

Less than two minutes later, they arrived at the chamber that had been described in the note. There were two torches, one on each of the side walls, providing sufficient light. On the far side of this small chamber, were the entrances to the four individual tunnels. And just like the note had said, each of their names, written on wooden boards, were nailed above the four tunnels.

Neil's name was above the tunnel on the far left. Nicola's was beside his. Then Claire's and finally Peter's.

Some light was emanating from each tunnel, so at least they weren't going to have to trek through them in darkness.

"Okay, now I am officially scared," Neil said, gulping.

"If you're scared," Claire said softly. "Then I am way, way scared." She held her hands out to show how badly they were shaking.

Neil took both of her hands: they were ice cold. That was partially due to the fact that it was cold down in these chambers, but also due to human physiology. (He vaguely remembered hearing somewhere that it is was part of each human's "fight or flight" response.)

"The longer we wait, the more scared we'll get," Nicola said.

"Yup," Peter remarked, agreeing with her completely. "Let's go and get this over with."

Peter walked and stood at his tunnel's entrance. Each member of his team, despite how unbelievably terrified they were, went to their tunnels as well.

"I know this is not the correct thing to say," Peter said with a smile, "but see you all on the other side." He giggled at his poor choice of phrase. "Anyway, you know what I mean."

CHAPTER 27

Neil's teeth chattered as he nervously walked down his tunnel. He wasn't consciously attempting to measure its length, but made a ballpark estimate that it was between twenty and thirty meters long. It gently curved to the left the entire time, which made it that much harder to guess how long it was. As he got further and further along, he finally spotted the "room" at the end. It was a lot smaller than he had expected. It was only a meter deep, and a meter and a half wide. The four doors, which had large yellow numbers painted on them, were significantly narrower than typical doors. And there was only a five-centimeter gap between each one: just enough space for the door jams.

"Yikes," Neil said to himself, feeling somewhat claustrophobic. He bent down to pick up the single white envelope which contained his unique riddle: the one which he now had to solve... by himself... with no help... double yikes.

Neil,

The 1,2,3,4 on the doors represent January 1st, 2nd, 3rd, and 4th. Imagine that today is January 4th. What day was the day before yesterday's tomorrow?

HI READER! (^_^)
BEFORE READING ON, SEE IF YOU CAN FIGURE OUT NEIL'S RIDDLE!
GOOD LUCK!

Neil paused. He had just read through the entire note without taking in a single word of it. "C'mon, man," he said to himself, slapping his cheeks a couple times. "Pull yourself together."

He reread the note, a lot slower this time. He enunciated every word carefully, even pausing when he got to the commas and period.

He now fully understood what the riddle was asking, but Neil felt it was going to require some math skills to solve, and math was not one of Neil's strengths. And his confidence in solving math word problems was almost non-existent.

"I've got no hope unless I write this down," he mumbled to himself.

Following Peter's advice, (well, it was actually Peter's *order*) Neil had kept the paper and pencil that he had used at Mr. Winchester's home. He sat down, leaned against the wall, and wrote "*1, 2, 3, 4*," from left to right on the page. Then he put his pencil on the *4*.

"Yesterday's tomorrow," he said slowly, "would be today." As soon as he finished saying that, he moved his pencil to the *3* and then returned it to the *4*. "So we are still on January 4th. And the day before that," he said while moving the pencil one number to the left, "is the 3rd."

Neil looked up at the door with the *3* on it.

"Pete told me to make sure I was TOTALLY sure before touching a knob," he said aloud. "I better to this again."

Neil went through the same thing one more time, and once again ended up with his pencil on the *3*.

"Alright," he said. "Now comes the moment of truth." He walked up, grabbed the cold doorknob of door 3 and twisted it. It opened, revealing a tunnel behind it.

"Yessss!" he said loudly while pumping his fist. "The Neilster is the man!"

* * *

Nicola's nerves were fairly under control as she walked down her tunnel. Her tunnel was a little longer than Neil's (but she had no way of knowing that...) and was straight for the first half, and then gently curved to the left for the second half.

"What a tiny room," she said as she entered the little chamber with the four doors in it.

"Ah, Mr. Note," she said to the envelope as she picked it up off the ground. "What bizarre riddle do you have in store for me?"

With a reasonable amount of confidence, she took out the note and read it to herself, slowly and silently:

Nicola,

The 1,2,3,4, on the doors represent 1st place, 2nd place, 3rd place, and 4th place in a 100-meter dash. The four participants in this race are Christopher, Anthony, Jason, and Robert.

Christopher, who is usually the fastest by far, couldn't pull off the win this time.

Anthony got off to a spectacular start, but ran out of gas toward the end.

Jason had a great race, and even though he beat Christopher by a nose, he didn't win.

Robert ran, quite possibly, the best race of his entire life. But he saw Christopher pass him just before he crossed the finish line.

What place was Robert?

HI AGAIN READER! (^_^)
IF YOU ENJOYED TRYING TO FIGURE OUT NEIL'S RIDDLE, WHY DON'T YOU GIVE NICOLA'S RIDDLE A SHOT, TOO?

"Talk about a long riddle," she muttered to herself, after reading the whole thing. "It's more like an essay. I'm going to have to re-enact this one in order to figure it out."

Since Nicola was not a six-year-old girl anymore, she did not carry around a bunch of dolls in her bag which she could have used as the "racers." But she did, of course, have some paper that she could tear into pieces, fold in half, and then place on the ground so they "stood up." She also took out her pencil and wrote "C, A, J, R" on the folded papers. Then she placed her bag on the ground a meter or so away, to use as a makeshift finish line.

Nicola lined the four boys up along the wall, imagining it as their start line.

"What I need to do is begin with the clues that contain at least two names," she said.

She began with the Jason clue, and picked up the two people it referred to, *Jason* and *Christopher*. "Well, all I know for sure is that Jason finished ahead of Christopher," she said. She put *Jason* about five centimeters away from the finish line, and *Christopher* five centimeters behind him.

Then she moved onto the Robert clue, as it also contained two names. "It says Christopher passed Robert before the finish line," she said softly. "That's just another way of saying Robert finished after Christopher." She placed *Robert* about five centimeters behind *Christopher*.

She looked at the position of the three "sprinters." Currently, Jason was in first, Christopher in second, and Robert in third. Now she had to deal with Anthony.

"I need to go through the other two clues," she said, "really, really carefully."

Just then, she felt a cold and sudden burst of wind.

"Oh?" she said with surprise. "Maybe someone just figured out their clue and opened the right door. That would've caused a little gust of wind due to a slight change in air pressure."

She turned back to her racers. "The first clue says Christopher didn't win," she said, wanting to double-check that she hadn't made any mistakes. "And I have him in second place right now, so that works."

Then she picked up Anthony. "Sounds like Anthony was leading at the start," she continued, "but ran out of juice. So that means he finished either second or third or fourth."

She reread the Anthony clue. "But how do I figure out which of those he was?" she asked herself. "I mean, it doesn't say."

Nicola held onto *Anthony*, and calmly read all four clues again. "I'm missing something here," she said. "And probably something, like, crazily obvious."

She sat down and leaned against the wall, reading the clues "ridiculously slowly" this time. (This was a technique that Peter had taught her ages ago...) Then she spotted it. "Got it!" she yelled. "The Jason clue says that he DID NOT win. And I currently have him in first. That can mean only one thing, then. Anthony won! Or did he... yeah, he must have! Bingo!!"

She placed *Anthony* down so he was against the edge of her bag. Then in a silly, deep, "broadcaster" voice, held up her pencil to her mouth like a microphone and announced, "What a final! But we'll have to wait for the photo replay to confirm the outcome. Hold on, everyone..." She paused a bit, giggled at herself, and then continued, "The results are now in! Anthony takes the gold! Jason the silver! Christopher the bronze! And Robert comes in an unfortunate fourth."

She kept giggling after finishing this announcement, since this type of silly behavior was very "un-Nicola" like. Her giggle then escalated into an all-out roaring laugh.

When her laughing fit finally ended, she stood up and picked up her bag. She strode confidently over to door four. "Sorry, Bob. Oops, I mean, Robert," she said. "But every race has to have its loser." She grabbed the doorknob of door 4 and twisted it... a tunnel! She'd done it!

* * *

Claire was terrified beyond words as she slowly shuffled her way down her tunnel. Hers began the same as Nicola's, going straight for the first half. Then it veered to the right just past the halfway point.

By the time she reached the tiny room with the four doors, her heart was pounding so hard that it hurt. She felt faint and dizzy, almost like she was about to pass out. This feeling was a first for her, as she was always overflowing with confidence when she captained the volleyball team in Grade 9.

She sat down on the cold stone floor, crossed her legs and closed her eyes. She knew she needed to calm herself down before even picking up the envelope.

It took over three minutes, but after a series of deep breaths, she'd managed to get her pulse rate back under eighty. (She knew it was eighty because she measured it by counting the number of beats in fifteen seconds with a couple fingers from her left hand on the inside of her right wrist, and then multiplying that number by four.) Her usual resting pulse rate was under sixty—which she knew from being an athlete—but eighty was low enough for now, all things considered.

The envelope which lay on the floor just to her right threatened to drive her heart rate up again, but she mentally refused to let it do so.

"Not this time," she said to herself strongly. "You've got this, Claire. You're in charge."

She removed the note and read the message aloud:

Claire,

The 1,2,3,4 on the doors represent the time span of 1 hour, 2 hours, 3 hours, and 4 hours.

You went to bed at 11:00 p.m. and you set your alarm for 5:00 a.m. the next morning. After an hour of staring at the ceiling, wide awake, you decided to change your alarm to go off an hour later. Then you slept like a baby for a while, but woke up three hours before your alarm was going to ring. You tossed and turned and tossed and turned and didn't get back to sleep until the time you had originally set your clock to go off. The next time you woke up was when your alarm starting ringing.

How many hours, in total, did you sleep for that night?

HI AGAIN READER! (^_^)
IF YOU ENJOYED TRYING TO SOLVE THE PREVIOUS TWO RIDDLES, WHY DON'T YOU TRY TO SOLVE CLAIRE'S AS WELL?

Claire rolled her eyes. "Why," she asked herself, "did my riddle have to be a novel instead of just a sentence or two? This is like one of those bonus questions that Mr. Zalasky puts at the end of his math tests. The ones that no one; well, no one other than Pete, ever manages to get right."

Claire put the note in her back pocket and then began stretching. Yes, stretching. Claire was both an athletic and academically talented young woman. She was also a strong believer in the mind-body connection. So Claire knew when her body felt good and relaxed, that her mind was more efficient. And vice versa. By getting her shoulders, back, legs, and neck a little more limber, she was expecting her mind to get super-charged to solve this riddle.

While stretching, she heard something. Soon after the noise, she felt a short, cold burst of air. "That must mean either Nik, Neil or Pete just opened the right door in their room," she said. Her comment threatened to drive her pulse up again, but she nipped it in the bud. "No way, brain," she ordered herself. "I'm the boss right now."

Claire took out her pencil and paper and leaned against one of the walls in the most comfortable way possible. First, she drew a long straight line on her page. Then she put little ticks on the lines every few centimeters, which were each going to represent a specific time. She wrote *11:00* at the far left of the line, *12:00* above the first tick to the right, *1:00* above the next tick, and continued until the end of the line, where she wrote *6:00*.

All I've gotta do," she said to herself, "is read it slowly. I'll draw wavy lines for awake hours and zigzag ones for asleep hours. It can't be that hard."

Claire tediously read each sentence three times, which was another technique Peter had taught her. (Peter had told her that careful people double-check, but perfectionists triple-check).

Once she was done all the reading and line drawing, she ended up with:

A wavy line from 11:00 to 12:00.
A zigzag line from 12:00 to 3:00.
A wavy line from 3:00 to 5:00.
A zigzag line from 5:00 to 6:00.

"Three hours here plus one hour there," she said to herself, "totals four." She looked up at door 4, back down at her paper, and then at the door again. "Sorry Petey, but I ain't triple checking my triple-checked answer." She giggled at that comment. "If I had needed to check each and every math problem this many times, I never would have had enough time to finish the easy math tests we did back in Grade 2!"

But then, she started rethinking what to do… Did it need to be looked at one more time??

"Claire, you know you're right," she said loudly, like she was being her own coach. She whistled while walking up to door 4, heart racing again. But this time it was from excitement rather than nervousness. She opened the door and looked at the tunnel on the other side.

"Yeah!" she said in a deep, loud voice, just like she always did after hitting a blistering spike in a volleyball match.

CHAPTER 28

Peter's tunnel slowly curved to the right from start to finish. Of course, Peter couldn't *just walk*—as that would be way too boring—so he began counting his steps, a habit that seemed to happen for him as unconsciously as blinking or breathing.

When he reached the room at the end, he paused for a few seconds before actually entering it.

"Wow," he said softly. "This certainly wasn't what I was expecting."

Peter had figured that since the majority of the rooms and chambers of the old ruins here at Silverhead Mountain had always been quite large and grand, that his "room with four doors" was going to be big as well.

"This place is tiny," he said.

The tininess was surprising, but the most bizarre thing was that it looked as if a kindergartener had been given a piece of yellow chalk and told to write the alphabet on the walls. The letters, each of which were written numerous times, were all jumbled up and in various sizes and locations. (Of course, a kid hadn't written them, but whoever did must have been half asleep, as very few were straight.) Many were written sideways or on angles, and some were even upside-down. It reminded Peter of the "pasta in a can" his dad used to serve them when his mom went out for dinner with friends. There was no easier way of "cooking" than just dumping two cans of that alphabet pasta stuff in a bowl, setting the microwave for two and a half minutes, and pressing start. But hey, kids would never complain, they loved the stuff.

He slapped his cheeks twice. "Pete, stay focused," he said to himself. Peter's overly active mind could be flipped on a dime. This was apparently another common symptom of ADHD.

"Pete, the puzzle," he said to himself. "Right now, it's all about the puzzle."

He picked up the envelope, taking deep breaths while doing so, and then closed his eyes as he removed the note.

"They are all counting on you," he said, eyes still shut. "You are NOT going to let them down."

He opened his eyes and looked at the very short note.

$$A \rightarrow A = 2$$
$$I \rightarrow I = 4$$
$$Y \rightarrow Y = ?$$

HI READER! (^_^)
WELL, PETER'S RIDDLE IS DEFINITELY HARDER TO FIGURE OUT THAN THE OTHER THREE, BUT EVERYONE LOVES A GOOD CHALLENGE, DON'T THEY? HAVE A GO AT THIS ONE, IF YOU DARE!

"What the…?" he said loudly, flabbergasted at what he was looking at.

"They've obviously given me the most confusing one to solve," he grumbled. "The losers… well, I'll show them who's the boss."

"First things first," he said to himself. "Clearly the answer has something to do with the letters A, I, and Y. So I might as well start by counting how many of each has been written on the walls."

"Four A's, nine I's, and six Y's," he said after counting. He tried to conjure up a way to apply some math here. "Hold on," he said, "There are 4 A's. If I divide 4 by 2, I get 2. Let me think… so what if I try dividing the number of I's by 2 as well? 9 I's, divided by 2, would equal 4.5, right?

He paused before continuing. "But in theory, if I ignore the digit to the right of the decimal point, then I'd have 4, exactly like it says in the clue. And then for the Y's, of which there are 6, if I divide that by 2, I get 3."

Peter looked at door 3. "Hey, door three!" he said loudly to it. "Are you the real thing?"

But Peter was not satisfied with his first attempt at a solution.

"Maybe I counted wrong," he said to himself. "Maybe there are only 8 *I's*, in which case my theory would be more solid.

Peter did a recount. Not only did he double-check the number of *I's*, but he did the same for the other two letters as well. And to ensure he didn't count each one more than once, he took out a chocolate bar from his backpack, and drew a "chocolate slash" through each one as he counted them.

"Nope," he said when he was done. "Same as the first count. Well, when Plan A doesn't work, go to Plan B."

Peter was referring to a saying Mr. Jacobson, his Grade 8 science teacher, used to say all the time. In other words, if your first idea is wrong, just try something else!

Peter paced around the room, even though there was very, very little space to actually "pace" in. He kept reciting the contents of the short note, substituting in the word "something" for the arrows.

"Think it through, Pete," he said to himself. *A* something *A* equals 2. *I* something *I* equals 4. *Y* something *Y* equals..."

When this led to nothing, without even breaking stride, he switched to reciting, "Four *A's*, nine *I's*, six *Y's*. Four *A's*, nine *I's*, six *Y's*."

His legs and mouth stopped almost simultaneously. "Hold on," he said very suddenly, as if he was finally onto something. "This might have to do with how each letter sounds. *I's* sounds like *eyes*, right? And *Y's* sound like *whys*... But wait, the number of *whys* can't be counted, can they?"

Peter's frustration level was on the rise. His first idea had been "okay," but not solid enough. And his second one was worthless. If there had been anything on the floor to kick, like a box or something, he would have taken his frustration out on it. He took a couple of breaths and tried to talk himself down.

"C'mon Pete, you know what to do. Option C," he said, thinking about Mr. Jacobson again.

But before contemplating what to do next, he needed to get those first two ideas completely out of his mind. He lay down flat on the ground and spread his arms and legs out. He closed his eyes and pictured "a smiling Mr. Winchester who had just been rescued by Peter and his team." He was thoroughly enjoying this image and wanted to continue thinking about it, but a brick floor in winter was not the ideal place for rest.

He opened his eyes and looked up at the ceiling. Then he twisted his neck sideways and looked over at the messy letters on the walls again.

Peter then jumped up. (Well, as fast as an inflexible kid with poor coordination skills can...) He closed his eyes again, as keeping them closed made it much easier to create better mental pictures.

"Yes," he said softly once. "Yes... YES!!" he yelled. "Option C! You are the one!"

Peter had just completed the triple-check in his mind, so he didn't need to wait another second. He grabbed the doorknob which he knew was going to open to the tunnel, and twisted it with zero doubt.

"Hello, Mr. Dark Tunnel," he said proudly while entering it. "Yes. Yes! Yes!!" he yelled again, jumping excitedly as he headed to reunite with his team.

CHAPTER 29

"Hey, listen to that," Neil said to Claire and Nicola, "I can hear Pete coming!"

"Pete, we all made it!" Nicola yelled well before Peter was within sight.

"I'm coming, ya'll," Peter yelled back with a hillbilly accent. "I don't wanna trip me-self, so I'm just takin' it slow!"

As soon as Peter got there, all four pulled each other in close for a long, strong group hug.

"We totally have to tell each other what our riddles were," Peter began. "I mean, I gotta hear about the ones you guys just figured out. But not right now. First, we gotta get this last challenge done and dusted, and rescue Bradley and Mr. Winchester. Then we can compare away until our hearts are content!"

Although he hadn't planned it that way, Peter's speech had been just what was needed: both a display of respect and admiration for his teammates, and a reminder that they weren't quite finished yet.

"Well," Neil said, pointing at the yellow arrow on the floor. "At least we don't have to guess how to get to the final challenge, do we?"

The arrow pointed to the entrance of another tunnel, one that looked much older and narrower than the ones they had just come through. Plus this tunnel appeared to be in very, very bad shape.

They could only see a couple of dimly burning torches along the walls, which meant they'd barely be able to see anything while walking through it.

"Let's take the two torches from this room with us," Claire suggested. "You know, it would be like carrying medieval flashlights."

"Nice thinking," Nicola said, giving her a high-five.

"Okay, how about this?" Neil added. "Pete and I will hold the torches. I'll go first, and we walk in single file, very slowly. Pete takes the rear."

"Perfect," Peter said. "That way you can pick the safest route, and I'll be able to light it up well enough for Claire, Nik, and I to see where we are stepping.

The two torches in the chamber weren't fixed to the walls: they were just resting in some type of holder. Removing them was pretty easy.

"Dudes," Neil said, holding his torch up high. "Don't you think what we are about to do would look cool in a movie?"

Everyone laughed.

"Not just *what we are about to do*," Nicola remarked. "I'd say the last few years, you know, all the crazy stuff going on with Zoltan and Xavier and the challenges would turn into a massively successful movie series!"

"You bet it would!" Peter exclaimed.

"I wonder which Hollywood hunk would play me?" Neil asked, trying to keep a straight face.

Everyone burst into laughter again.

"Okay, sorry to rain on your parade," Peter said, bringing everyone back to reality. "But let's go rescue my brother and Mr. Winchester. We can talk more about movie rights and being famous later."

"Roger, captain," Neil said, saluting Peter.

"Neil," Claire said, shaking her head. "You are the WEIRDEST person I've ever met."

"Or will ever meet," Neil replied quickly, giving her a kiss on the cheek.

Mood now lightened again, it was time to start moving. Neil took his first step into what looked like was going to be a very difficult tunnel to navigate.

CHAPTER 30

The tunnel was way longer and in much worse shape than they ever could have imagined. When they got to a spot about halfway along, they noticed that so much of the ceiling and walls had collapsed that they actually had to climb up and over the rubble. They needed to wriggle through a gap that was no more than sixty centimeters wide.

* * *

When they finally made it to the end of the tunnel, everyone other than Peter—who was already worrying about what was next—breathed a sigh of relief.

"That tunnel was brutal, man," Neil said. "Look at my left hand, and my knees."

Since Neil had been leading the way and holding a torch with one hand, he had slipped, tripped, fallen over, and skidded several times. The palm of his left hand had a few scrapes on it that were bleeding. And the knees of his jeans were ripped on both legs, and some blood was visible there too.

"We'd better disinfect those," Peter said, reaching into his backpack.

"Don't tell me you brought your entire medicine cabinet with you?" Neil joked. "Pete and his bottomless backpack!"

"Just sit still," Peter instructed him. "And close your eyes."

First, he took out his water bottle, which was still eighty percent full, and poured some water over Neil's hand and knees.

"That wasn't too bad," Neil said, opening his eyes and preparing to stand up.

"Sit down, dude," Peter said to him with a grin. "I'm just getting started."

"Looks like your future husband may be interested in becoming a physician," Claire whispered to Nicola while nudging her a couple of times. She had said it quietly enough that only Nicola had heard her, and the reddening of Nicola's face indicated that perhaps she'd already pictured herself married to Peter one day.

Peter then took out a small hand towel, and dabbed Neil's hand and knees a few times to soak up the excess water.

"Okay, now comes the disinfecting part," Peter explained. "This might sting. A lot. But if I don't do it, your scratches might get infected. Nik and

Claire, hold his shoulders so he doesn't try to squirm away."

Neil shut his eyes. That was lucky for him, as it meant he didn't see Peter remove the bottle of iodine and box of cotton swabs from his backpack. He took a swab, turned the bottle upside-down and waited until the iodine had soaked it sufficiently, and got ready to start. He held Neil's left wrist very firmly and began dabbing the scratches with the iodine-soaked swab.

"Weeouch!" Neil yelped in a high-pitched voice, trying his best to yank his hand away.

Peter said nothing in response. He just tightened his grip and got back to work. Once he was confident that he had disinfected Neil's hand sufficiently, he prepared a fresh swab and got started on the right knee first, and then the left.

Neil yelped, squirmed, wriggled, and even begged for Peter to, "Please just stop!" But Peter was focused. Totally focused.

"There you go, sir," Peter said once his work was done. "No need to worry about those scratches anymore."

Neil jumped up and walked a few steps away. It sounded like he was saying some four-letter words, but even if he was; no one could make them out. (But Peter also did the same thing every time his mom used iodine on his cuts.) Having a cut disinfected was no fun, but was necessary.

Pride somewhat damaged, but hand and knees now safe from infection, Neil walked back over to join his friends. As he was approaching them, a series of torches "magically" lit up all over the room they had recently entered. The light revealed what could be described as no less than magnificent. Unfortunately, magnificent in a bad way...

CHAPTER 31

What they were looking at was so fascinating and mysterious that all four of them were speechless.

They were standing on some sort of ledge, which was about three meters long and a meter and a half wide. The ledge dropped off into a huge dark pit. When they peered over the ledge to see how far it went down, there was no bottom in sight.

The ledge on the opposite side of the pit looked to be at least five or six meters away.

The opposite ledge itself had only two things of importance on it. The first was an archway, which likely led to a tunnel, and ultimately to where Bradley and Mr. Winchester were being held. And the second was what appeared to be a drawbridge, like the kind you'd find at medieval castles. (Back in those times, the only way to gain entrance to a castle was to have the drawbridge lowered over the moat.) The drawbridge they were looking at now was connected firmly to the opposite ledge, and was being held in a near-vertical position by thick chains which disappeared into holes in the stone ceiling.

But it was what was on their side that was the most bizarre. There were numerous stone blocks, each about half the size of a shoebox. Each block was hanging on the end of a long chain. And similar to the drawbridge, these chains also disappeared into the ceiling above. Plus, each dangling block had a yellow number or symbol on it.

"Dudes," Neil said nervously. "This is, like, really, uh…"

The other three didn't know how to help Neil finish his sentence, as they all felt the same way as he did. Peter walked closer to the hanging blocks. While he did that, Neil and Claire went up to the walls, where numerous incomplete mathematical equations had been written in yellow on both sides.

"We've got all the numbers, zero through nine," Peter said while checking out the blocks. "A decimal point. A plus sign. A minus sign. A multiplication sign. A division sign. And an equals sign."

"What is this place?" Neil asked jokingly. "A mathematician's paradise? Or a torture chamber for people who suck at arithmetic?"

"And what do you make of all these equations on the walls?" Nicola asked. "Like, this one says

8x4=, and that one says *3.2+8=*, but none of them have the answers written."

"No kidding, eh," Claire remarked. "It looks like a Grade 4 math test!"

They had been so preoccupied with the drawbridge, hanging blocks, and wall equations, that none of them had noticed the envelope on the floor. It wasn't until Neil stepped on it accidentally that they became aware of its existence.

"Oh," he said, sounding a little surprised. "So there is a note this time." He pulled the note out of the envelope and read it aloud.

Your final challenge! You're almost there! (But as we all know, in this game, ALMOST means nothing...)

Allow us to explain your final challenge:

You must pull on ten of these hanging blocks, in the correct order, to trigger the drawbridge to lower.

You have 3 attempts. For each attempt, you can pull on each block only once. (Just in case you weren't reading slowly enough, if you pull the same block twice during an attempt, you automatically fail that attempt.)

You will know if you have made a mistake because a loud buzzer will sound. After it sounds, the blocks that you pulled down will shift back up to their original positions. Then you may start your next attempt.

Now I suppose you want a hint as to how to figure this out...

Well, you are a pretty clever group. Or at least that's what you'd like to think, right?

So you don't need any more hints, do you? Just look around!

"Yikes," Neil said without thinking. "This is N-O-T going to be easy."

"Certainly isn't," Peter said. "But think about how many times we have felt like this before." He paused, as a way to prepare to ram home his point. "And out of all those times, how many did we end up failing?"

"Zero!" Nicola said loudly.

"You got it!" Neil yelled. "A big, fat, gross, stinky zero!"

"Neil," Claire said, a little shocked by Neil's crudeness, "I don't think zeroes can be big, or fat, or gross, or—"

"Neilster!" Peter said, catching everyone by surprise. "You may use any and all adjectives you please to describe that Z-E-R-O!"

"I bet I know what you're planning to say next," Nicola said, looking at Peter.

"Be my guest, beautiful," he said, encouraging her to finish his speech for him.

"You're gonna say something like *if we've always done it before, then we're gonna do it again.*"

"Well, something like that," Peter admitted. "But I was also going to add one thing to that."

"Which is?" Claire asked.

Peter took a deep breath, exhaled it, and then got a very serious expression on his face. "Bradley and Mr. Winchester are depending on us," he said. "We can't let them down. I cannot, I will not, allow that to happen."

"Then let's do this!" Neil said confidently, putting his hands out for everyone to receive high-fives.

"Yeah," Peter said with vigor. "Game on!"

CHAPTER 32

"Pete," Nicola said, "I don't mean to put any pressure on you, but... uh... where, or, uh... how do we start?"

"Yeah, you're the math man, dude," Neil said, slapping Peter on the back.

Peter smiled and took a few seconds to look at each member of his team. They all respected and admired him, and even more importantly, they were also kind people and genuine friends.

"I do indeed like math," he said, feeling his voice starting to get shaky. "But not even a *fraction* as much as I like you three." His lips were now quivering, an unintentional display of how emotional he was. "I will... do... whatever I can to solve this. I've got to. But I need you three to have my back. Wait, that sounded a little weird, didn't it?"

Peter's word choice was not the best, but he had effectively made his point.

"Your request is our command," Neil said. "Wait, that's not right... Your wish is our... C'mon, what's that expression again?"

Comical Neil, though completely by accident, had once again managed to lighten the mood. Good on him.

"I'm currently only in the brainstorming stage of this puzzle," Peter replied. "But seeing as how there is a *times*, *divided by*, *plus*, *minus*, *equals*, and *decimal point*, I think we can be safe in assuming that we need to make a math equation. And in all likelihood, one that is mathematically sound."

"Oh," Nicola said. "You mean, like 1+2×3=9, right? Oh wait, that only uses seven blocks, so that wouldn't work. But you know what I mean."

"Umm..." Peter said, eyes looking upward and to the left: something that not only Peter did, but most humans do while thinking. "Well, both yes and no. Yes to the fact that we have to use ten blocks. But no to the fact that your example was mathematically wrong."

"Wrong?" Nicola asked. "1+2 is 3, right? And 3×3 is 9."

"Ah, I think I get what he's after," Neil commented. "Don't you all remember when Mrs. Baird taught us *P.E.M.D.A.S.* in Grade 7?"

"Good old pemdas," Peter smiled, "is exactly what I'm referring to. You know, the order of operations: Parenthesis, exponents, multiplication, division, addition, subtraction. Remember that when doing a calculation, multiplication and division must be done before addition and subtraction."

"Oh, I remember that now," Nicola said. "So I should have done 2×3 first, which is 6. Then added 1, for a total of 7."

"Yup," Peter answered.

"It's going to be confusing to create one that will work, don't you think?" Neil asked.

"Without any clues, it would be," Peter answered. "But look at the walls. That's where the hints are. We just have to, well... find them, I guess. I can't tell you where to start looking, as I don't really know."

"That's what we are here for, Petey," Neil said. "We'll look at numbers on the wall on your behalf."

Another senseless comment from Neil, but they all laughed a little. Good on him, again.

Thankfully, they all still had their papers and pencils with them. Plus, Peter reached in his backpack and handed them all erasers.

"Is there anything you didn't bring?" Neil joked. "I'd love for you to whip out four calculators next!"

"I wish," Peter smiled. "I only wish." But Peter had the absolute worst poker face in the world, so everyone knew instantly that he was hiding something.

"You do have a calculator in there, don't you?" Nicola said playfully, pinching the back of Peter's neck.

Now quite red-faced, Peter reached into his backpack again and triumphantly pulled out his calculator.

"Petey," Neil remarked. "You are a true mystery. I can't even imagine why anyone would carry a calculator around with them."

"Good," Peter replied, "'Cause I wasn't planning on telling you anyway."

More laughter.

He placed the calculator on the ground near the entrance. "Since I only brought one," he said, "I'll leave it here. And anyone can use it whenever they want."

"And I suppose *you* will be doing all the math in your head, right?" Claire asked Peter.

"*All* the math, no," he answered. Then he winked once. "But most of it, yes."

They each set out to look more closely at the walls, pencils and papers in hand. There were so many equations to look at that they literally could start anywhere.

Basically, they were all doing the same type of thing: calculating the answers of any two of the incomplete equations, and then seeing how (or if) they could add or subtract those two numbers to produce an answer that didn't use any digit more than once.

* * *

About ten minutes after beginning—which was way too much math for anyone other than Peter—they noticed Claire walk over and pick up the calculator again. Since it wasn't the first time she had done so, neither Peter nor anyone else reacted. They just kept thinking through their own ideas.

"Guys!" she yelled. "I think I've got it! Look! 3×9=27. And 84÷7=12. I just confirmed that one on Pete's calculator. So if we take 27, and subtract 12 from it, we get 15. Look, the math works. And no digit is used more than once."

Peter looked quickly over her math.

$$3 \times 9 - 84 \div 7 = 15$$

"You got it, babe!" Peter yelled excitedly.

"Excuse me, fine sir," Neil said, bumping Peter lightly in the hip. "Please leave the referring to Claire as *babe* to me, her boyfriend."

That comment sure got all of them laughing.

"Claire," Peter said, "Awesome job! Please do the honors, and pull the blocks in that order."

She handed her paper to Peter and walked up to the *3*. She pulled it and noticed it came down about ten centimeters. Then they heard a loud click from somewhere in the ceiling. She let go of the block, and it remained in its new lower position.

"No buzzer!" Neil said happily. "We are golden!"

"Next, the multiplication sign," Peter told Claire.

She walked over and pulled the "×" block. It came down just like the *3* had, and was followed by another click from above. But right after the click, a loud buzzer went off, startling all of them. Then both of the blocks she had pulled down returned to their original positions.

"What?" Neil said in confusion. "Why?

Peter looked down at the paper again. The math was right. It should be working.

Nicola politely asked Peter if she could take a look at Claire's notes, without saying exactly why. A few seconds later, she looked up at the other three. "I'm afraid," she explained, "we overlooked, or maybe I should say *missed*, a little error in Claire's solution. Hers requires eleven blocks to be pulled, not ten. I just counted carefully. Twice. Look."

Peter quickly snatched the paper back and counted for himself. "Oops," he announced. "My bad. I should have spotted that."

"No, Pete," Claire said, "I made the mistake, not you."

"It wasn't a mistake," Peter said, patting a deflated Claire on the back. "And think of it this way, we now know the first block in the solution is the *3*, right?"

CHAPTER 33

"You're just trying to make me feel better, even though I screwed up," Claire remarked. "But for what it's worth, thanks."

"I was being totally serious," Peter replied quickly. "It's awesome that we now know the first block to pull. Knowing that eliminates so many possibilities."

"Oh, so... that did help?" Claire asked, perking up a little.

"Totally," Peter answered. "Alright guys, figure out an equation that starts with a 3. And remember that the *times* does not come right after the *3*."

They split up again and continued where they'd left off, but with a much narrower range of focus now. Surely someone would come up with the answer eventually. Another big plus they had on their side was the fact that no time limit was being imposed.

"Pete," Neil said, walking up beside him. "I know I'm the worst at math by far, but... well..."

"Let's hear it," Peter said supportively. "And you don't suck at math. You just never do your homework. That's why you make so many careless mistakes on your tests."

"Never thought of it that way," Neil replied, a tad more energized than before that compliment. "Okay, it seems like we are all trying to create a long equation where the equals sign is near the end. You know, like $A+B \times C \div D=$. But when I look at all the stuff written on the walls, everything is something like $A+B=$ or $C \times D=$. So that got me thinking. What if we try to find two equations on the walls that produce the same answer? Then all we have to do is put the *equals sign* in the middle of the equation."

During Neil's long and academic-sounding speech, both Claire and Nicola had gravitated a little closer, out of curiosity.

"That certainly could work," Peter replied. "I like your thinking. Let's give it a go. Not only is your plan very feasible, it's also much easier than what we've been doing up till now."

They split up for a third time, writing down every equation and the answer to each one. Peter had given each person on his team a specific section of the wall to do, so he knew they wouldn't miss any. The plan was to compare papers and search for any matches as soon as they were ready.

* * *

About fifteen minutes later, they all sat down and put their papers side by side. Claire, drawing on her leadership skills, doled out some instructions. "Okay, Nik," she announced. "You take the calculator. Neil, you read the equations to her. This is how we are going to double-check that our answers are all correct. If any answer is wrong, say stop, and we'll change it."

Peter took advantage of this opportunity to calm himself down a little. His bad habit of catastrophizing was trying to come to the forefront of his mind, and he needed to push it away.

* * *

Of all the equations, of which there were around a hundred in total, only two had been calculated incorrectly. (And both of those were on Neil's page.)

"Okay, guys," Claire said. "Now all we have to do is scan until we find the same answer for two."

There was probably a more efficient way of doing this, but since they didn't feel like thinking up one, they just began randomly picking an answer, and then looking up and down the other pages for a match.

"I found one!" Nicola shouted. "Look! This one on Pete's page and this one on Claire's. The answer for both is 15.5!"

They all leaned in close. "She's right," Claire said. "Now we just gotta make sure it uses ten, you know, ten blocks."

Peter wrote it down.

$$62 \div 4 = 3.1 \times 5$$

"Mathematically speaking," he said he a professor-like voice, "it works! And it requires exactly ten blocks!

"But wait," Nicola commented before anyone stood up to start pulling on the blocks. "It has to start with a 3, doesn't it?"

"Whew, thanks for reminding me," Peter said. He erased what he had just written and then wrote:

$$3.1 \times 5 = 62 \div 4$$

"Neil," Peter instructed, "since you were the one who got us started on the right track, you can be in charge of pulling the blocks this time. I'll read them out one by one."

"Roger that," Neil said, standing up and saluting Peter.

"Go, Neilster, go!" Claire called out.

The whole group smiled and laughed again.

"Okay, let's do this," Peter began. "Three."

Neil pulled the *3*, and they all heard the click.

"Decimal point," Peter said next.

Neil pulled that block, heard the click... No buzzer.

"One!" Peter said loudly.

Neil pulled the *1*. Just like the previous two blocks, it was correct.

"Multiplication sign!" Peter said loudly, unable to contain his excitement.

Neil remained calm, not wanting to screw this up. He walked over to the "×" block, double-checked to make sure it wasn't the "+" block, and pulled it. Another click. But then a loud buzzer! And then those four blocks moved back up to their original positions.

"What?!" Claire yelled. "Not again!"

"I pulled the right one!" Neil said, wanting to confirm he hadn't done anything wrong.

Peter, now visibly shaken up, started pacing around in a figure eight. His friends knew by now that pacing in a circle meant thinking, but a figure eight meant Peter was in a more panicked state. They also were worried that interrupting him with a comment, or even something as simple as a hug, could do more harm than good.

Nicola, Neil, and Claire sat down and leaned against the wall. They remained completely silent. They also avoided all eye contact with

Peter. They simply listened to the repetitive sound of his footsteps on the stone floor.

Now what??

CHAPTER 34

Peter was not intentionally avoiding his team, but he was completely in a world of his own. He just kept retracing his figure eight over and over, occasionally looking at the four papers or at the walls, and mumbling away indecipherably the whole time.

"How long does he usually do this?" Claire whispered to Neil at a volume that Peter definitely couldn't hear.

"For as long as he wants," Neil whispered back. "Could be a few minutes. Could be an hour."

"Yeah," Nicola added, also at a whisper. "And we've all learned by now that the best, well, the only thing to do when he gets like this is just wait it out. He'll either come up with the solution, or come back over here and ask for more help."

* * *

Peter looked at his watch. He had been pacing, non-stop, for twenty-seven minutes now. "What have I missed?" he said to himself for the umpteenth time. "Aargh… the ceiling?" He looked up at the ceiling, knowing it would probably yield nothing. "Nothing up there." And he also knew there was nothing on the floor. He had studied and studied the equations on the walls, but could find nothing new that would help.

And he had scanned through the four papers so thoroughly by now that he'd almost memorized everything on them. There were only two equations that produced the same answer.

He suddenly stopped pacing, which caused Neil, Nicola, and Claire to look up. Peter crushed the papers into a ball and angrily threw them toward the opposite ledge. It didn't even get close to reaching the target. It ended up falling down into the dark pit.

"Why did you do that, Pete?" Nicola asked, even though she wasn't sure if speaking now was advisable or not. "You figure something out?"

"NO!" Peter replied sharply. He paused for a few seconds before continuing. He reminded himself not to take his anger out on his team. "I'm sorry. I'm just angry. Not at you guys, at myself."

Peter's emotions could—and often did—change very quickly, and Nicola guessed that his anger was about to turn to despair. She jumped up and ran over to him.

"Pete," she said, forcing out a fake smile. "Don't worry."

"Don't worry" was probably the phrase that had been said to Peter more times than any other phrase in his entire life, especially when he was in elementary school. But Peter was NOT going let worry take over right now. Absolutely not.

"Don't worry, Nik," he replied. "'Cause I'm not worried at all. Sure, our first ideas haven't panned out. But we have not exhausted every single possibility. We'll figure this out, as a team."

"You bet!" Nicola said supportively, proud of the conviction in Peter's voice.

"Well, I'm glad we are all smiles again," Claire commented. "But, uh…what do we try next?"

"Should we read the note again?" Neil asked.

Peter's photographic memory didn't need to hear the note again. He knew EXACTLY what it said. But just because he had memorized its contents didn't mean the rest of his team had.

"Sure, sounds good," Peter said. "But before you start reading, remember this: We CAN figure this thing out. I promise you that. I, well, I guarantee it. As a team, we are invincible."

"Yeah," Nicola quickly followed. "So let's, like, imagine that we just walked in to start this challenge. You know, so someone reads the clue, and then we all start thinking, from scratch again. C'mon, with our talents, solving this puzzle will be as easy as pie!"

Peter put his hands on Nicola's shoulders and planted a big kiss right on her lips.

"Woohoo!" Neil shouted, having never seen Peter kiss Nicola before.

"You're, uh... welcome," Nicola said shyly, wiping the excess spit off her face, as Peter's kiss had inaccurately landed on part of her nose as well.

But upon closer inspection of his expression, it was clear that this wasn't just a "thank you for the encouragement" kiss.

"Pete," Nicola asked. "You've just figured it out, haven't you?"

"Maximilian, Aurora, Cynthia!" he yelled loudly. "You almost had us! But almost is NOT good enough!"

"Okay, so what did you just figure out?" Neil asked excitedly.

"Me?" Peter smiled. "Nothing, actually. Nik just figured it out for us."

"Neil, you've still got the note, right?" Peter asked.

"Yup," Neil replied, pulling it out of his back pocket.

"Then could you, kind sir," Peter said with a smile, "please read us the final two sentences?"

"Uh, okay," he said. "The last two are, uh... *So you don't need any more hints, do you? Just look around!*"

"Look around. AROUND. That's the clue!" Peter explained.

But his audience had no idea where this was going. "Okay, sorry guys," he said. "I'm not very good at explaining what's going on in my brain sometimes. The solution hit me when Nik was trying to console me. She said not to worry, and that we could start this challenge all over again, or something like that. And then she said, it would be as easy as pie. Pie! Or, well, what I should say is *Pi*. The equations on the walls were red herrings to try and fool us."

Since they had no idea that he was referring to the mathematical Pi, Peter had to continue his explanation.

"The answer is the numerical value of Pi," he went on. "You know, the number used when calculating anything to do with circles."

"Pi?" Nicola asked. "But isn't that just 3.14?"

"That's the truncated version they teach for the sake of simplicity at school," Claire said, helping Peter out. "You know, so we can get fairly accurate answers without using a calculator. But Pi actually continues infinitely." She paused. "But does anyone know the first ten digits? I think I remember a few more, but not that many."

"Sure," Neil said, very unexpectedly. "3.14159265."

"Wow!" Claire said to him. "Why do you know that?"

"Never underestimate the—" Neil began saying.

"Don't say Neilster!" Claire said loudly, cutting him off.

The laughter was back in their group again.

"Never underestimate the Neilster!" Peter yelled. "As the Neilster, the awesomely cool Neilster, is completely correct!"

Peter wrote Pi on a page and got ready to begin.

"Since this is our final attempt, we can't afford to accidentally pull the wrong one," he explained. "So here's how we'll do this: I will say the number. Nik will walk up to it. Then Claire and Neil will both say 'okay' before she pulls the block. No mistakes."

"Wait guys, wait," Claire said, looking over Peter's shoulder at the paper, with a concerned expression. "The numbers 1 and 5 are each used twice."

"Oh," Peter said, "you're right." His mood began to fall instantly.

"Not to worry," Neil announced before Peter got too deflated. "Look, there are actually two *1* blocks, one right here and one other there. And there are two *5* blocks as well!"

Peter looked up. "You're right, there are! How did I not notice that when we first came in here?"

Peter smiled from ear to ear. "Pi is definitely the solution," he announced. "Man, what a tricky puzzle!"

Peter began to say each number, and after an "okay" from Neil and Claire, Nicola pulled each block. As expected, the clicks were heard but the buzzer never went off.

When she pulled the tenth block, a *5*, the click was followed by a loud grinding noise. They watched in awe as the drawbridge slowly began to come down.

About a minute later, the top of the drawbridge clanked down on their side. They now had a bridge to walk across toward victory!

Peter gingerly put one foot on the bridge. It was very strong and sturdy.

"It's safe," he announced. "But go slowly, and don't look down."

With Peter leading the way, they all walked cautiously in single file. When all four were on the opposite ledge, high-fives and hugs began.

"There's the exit," Neil said, pointing at the archway they were heading toward. He paused. "But I bet Mr. Winchester and Bradley are probably locked in cells or something. And we'll likely have to find a way to break them out."

"Let's hope you're wrong," Peter said. "But even if you are right about that, we can deal with it. C'mon, guys. Let's finish up this rescue. I'm getting hungry!"

CHAPTER 35

As soon as they entered the archway, which was the entrance to another long tunnel, they immediately spotted a white envelope on the ground.

"Not another one!" Neil said with a great deal of irritation in his voice. "That challenge we just did was supposed to be the last one."

Peter, who was running on fumes now, didn't really know how to reply. He quickly picked up the envelope and took out the note. "Nik, please," he said.

Nicola knew that this meant, once again, Peter wanted her to read the note. Having no reason not to, she unfolded the note and began reading aloud.

Well done! You are quite the group!

We hope that was a lot of fun for you four, as it was certainly interesting for us to set up.

At the end of this long tunnel is an unlocked door, which opens to the room where Bradley and Mr. Winchester are awaiting your arrival. (And no, there are no tricks or traps between here and there.)

Congratulations! (We hope you can pick up the sarcasm in that comment, ha ha ha!)

And we shall likely be seeing all six of you (you four plus Bradley and Mr. Winchester) again sometime soon. Possibly a lot sooner than you are expecting!

Maximilian, Aurora, Cynthia

"What are they talking about?" Neil asked. "They'll see us again? Why?"

"No clue," Claire said.

"Hey Pete," Nicola commented. "Even though this note says there are no more tricks or traps, I am guessing that you are not going to take their word for it."

"Definitely not," Peter said. "Corridor technique, team. We take no chances."

"The what technique?" Claire asked. She hadn't been part of the original team two and a half years ago when they learned the corridor technique from Mr. Winchester. Nicola quickly explained how it worked, and that it was the only way to guarantee safe passage down long tunnels or paths like this.

"Okay, I think I get it," she said after hearing the explanation. "So I do Bradley's old role. I go last, facing backward, arms locked with Nik and Neil. And I look for anything behind us that seems out of place. If I don't see anything weird, I say 'clear,' and then we all take another step."

"You're a quick learner, babe," Neil remarked.

Although Claire guessed that Neil's comment was intended as a compliment, another part of her interpreted it as being somewhat sarcastic. She gave Neil the evil eye, something that he hadn't seen from her in at least a couple of months.

Peter noticed it and jumped in to do some damage control. "She's a very quick learner," Peter said. "Without her, we'd never have made it this far."

Neil winked at Peter. Nice save!

The corridor technique was painstakingly slow and tedious, but it made sure they got where they were headed without any surprises.

* * *

It took them a good fifteen minutes before they finally reached the door at the end of the tunnel. There had been no traps along the way, just as promised in the note. So at least they knew the last part of the note was truthful. But they had serious doubts about whether the rest of it was true...

Peter's heart was racing so fast now that he felt faint and dizzy. His imagination was running through so many ridiculous possibilities about what could be lying on the other side of the door. He even pictured Mr. Winchester and Bradley hooked up to some evil contraption, being slowly lowered into a vat of molten metal.

A racing heart, which was making his breaths short and rapid, didn't mix well with the huge amount of dust down here. This caused Peter to start wheezing a little. He quickly reached into his backpack and pulled out his inhaler. He used it twice, the maximum allowable for an acute asthma attack.

Crisis averted?

Peter's friends were all aware of his occasional asthma attacks and knew that usually, with the help of his inhaler, he'd be fine.

* * *

"Okay, thanks guys," Peter said once his wheezing was relieved and his breathing was back to normal. "I'm good to go."

CHAPTER 36

All four of them were blown away (figuratively, not literally!) when they opened the door to the room holding Mr. Winchester and Bradley. The room they had just entered couldn't have been any more different from what they'd imagined the "holding cell" to look like.

They were pleasantly surprised when Bradley and Mr. Winchester, who both looked perfectly healthy, were waiting for them with open arms as soon as they walked in. This, of course, led to a round of happy hugs and big cheers. Peter was extremely relieved that they had finally achieved what they had set out to do, but also suspicious about what was going on.

This "cell" had a large power generator in it, with a big mess of cables heading in two directions. One pile went to a series of six or seven televisions, which were lined up on three big folding tables. The other set of cables went to a fridge, microwave, and heater. Mr. Winchester's rocking chair (the actual one from his house) and a very comfy-looking sofa were set up so that the two "detainees" could comfortably watch TV.

Peter walked over to look at what each TV was showing, since they certainly weren't television shows. It didn't take long for him to put two and two together.

"These monitors," Peter said, "are showing all the locations from the cameras that Maximilian, Aurora, and Cynthia set up. The ones they put at all the spots we just did our challenges at."

"You are correct," Mr. Winchester said.

"B-b-but..." Peter mumbled, thinking (or at least trying to think) about what this all meant. He paused as his mind rapidly ran through possibilities. "Oh, I get it! They brought in the rocking chair and sofa so you could have front row seats to watch us struggle with the puzzles." He paused again. "And then they could watch your reactions first-hand, right? Which I assume was amazingly entertaining for them... well, until right before we came in here. 'Cause that's when they must have bolted, right?"

Mr. Winchester came over, put his arm around Peter's shoulder, and took him over to the sofa.

"Oh, Peter," he said. "That mind of yours really does go into overdrive sometimes, doesn't it?"

He urged Peter to take a seat, and then went and slowly sat down in his rocking chair.

Bradley remained standing, but Neil, Nicola, and Claire came over quickly and squished together on the sofa. They didn't want to miss a single word of this.

"After kidnapping myself and Bradley," Mr. Winchester began, "they brought us here, to, well, be spectators to today's challenges. But shortly after they put us in here, they took Zoltan, who they had trapped in a container similar to the one we had used on Xavier, and left."

"They what?" Neil asked. "You mean they weren't even watching?"

"Well, if they were," Mr. Winchester replied, "they weren't doing so from in here."

"But why?" Nicola asked. "I mean, I thought that people from Sevlar loved everything about puzzles. Wouldn't they want to… uh… look, sorry to change topics so quickly, but weren't those three sent to Earth to *help* Zoltan?"

"Supposedly, yes," Mr. Winchester responded. "But if they came to help Zoltan, then why would they trap him? And more importantly, why did they know *how* to trap him?"

"Hold on," Peter said. "Are you saying that they somehow secretly planned this from the start? I mean, it said so in a note they wrote for us, but I figured they were just trying to scare us or something."

"Peter," Mr. Winchester replied. "The more I think about it, the more confident I've become that there is only one logical explanation."

"Which is ??" Peter asked.

"Those three must be working for Xavier," Mr. Winchester said.

"Xavier!?" Peter blurted out. "But he's jailed back on Sevlar! He couldn't have communicated or coordinated such a scheme from there."

"Unfortunately," Mr. Winchester continued, "when Xavier returned to Sevlar trapped in that box, a lot of people, especially the younger generation, strongly objected to him being held as a criminal."

"How did you find all this out?" Claire asked.

Mr. Winchester hesitated. He looked either unsure of himself, or concerned whether his young friends were ready to hear what he was about to say.

"A couple days ago," he began, "I dropped a tiny recording device in the pocket of Maximilian's coat, as their suspicious behavior had been causing me many sleepless nights. I wish I had done so earlier, though. That way I might have had a chance to do something before it came to this. I heard them discussing everything: things like how many of the guards in charge of keeping Xavier captive are corrupt, and that Xavier now has more than six thousand followers and supporters."

"Hold up," Peter said. "The lead weather gods specifically chose those three to come to Earth, right? There's no way he could have corrupted the leaders!"

"Directly, no. But indirectly, it's definitely possible," Mr. Winchester replied. "I suspect that his followers threatened the lead weather gods. They could've said things like they would harm their families if they didn't select Maximilian, Aurora, and Cynthia."

"This is ludicrous," Peter said in a panic, standing up and walking around the room. "Okay, let's just assume, for now, that you're right. So they've got Zoltan. So that's that. They've taken him back to Sevlar, where Xavier gets to torture him or torment him or whatever. We, and by *we,* I mean the people of Earth, are really the ones who lose. We no longer have someone to control the weather."

"All true," Mr. Winchester replied.

"So it's over then," Peter said, sitting down. "I mean, we are no longer part of this. They don't need us anymore."

"But then why did that final note say that they would see us again soon?" Nicola asked.

"Unfortunately," Mr. Winchester said, slowly standing up. "I also had a feeling this wasn't over yet."

"I don't get it!" Peter said loudly. "Don't tell me they are planning to kidnap *us* next, take us to

Sevlar, and force us to make puzzles for their entertainment?"

"That would be like being their slaves," Claire said.

"No, nothing like that," Mr. Winchester replied. "Look, I'll explain it on the way. There is somewhere we have to go. But first, I need to talk to Peter in private."

"Why?" Bradley asked, looking at Mr. Winchester like he didn't trust him anymore.

"Settle down, Bradley," the old man said. "Okay, if that makes you uncomfortable, I will speak to Peter in the back seat of the car as we drive there. Neil, you will drive Peter and I. Bradley, you take the two girls."

"Where are we going?" Neil asked.

"To my shed," Mr. Winchester replied.

"Why?" Neil asked again.

"As I just said, I'll explain it to Peter on the way," Mr. Winchester answered. "Bradley, follow us closely. And just to prove you can trust me, I'll give you this to hold on to."

Mr. Winchester handed Bradley a small bag with a zipper on it, which was about the size of a wallet. "That's my December supply of medications," he told Bradley. "Without those, my risk of having a heart attack or stroke goes sky high."

Bradley felt a little guilty, but a little guilt now was better than a ton of regret later. He accepted the box.

"Hold on a sec," Claire said. "You just said Bradley's car, right? You mean that when they kidnapped you, they made you drive yourselves out here?"

"Yup," Bradley replied.

"But it wasn't in the parking lot," Nicola said. "You can't just, like, hide a car."

"I can't," Mr. Winchester said. "But weather gods sure can."

* * *

They retraced the path they had taken to get to the entrance to the ruins.

"Mr. Winchester," Nicola said, looking concerned. "How did you get all the way up here? You never could have climbed up this dangerous route."

"I didn't walk up here," he replied. "Maximilian used a little tornado to carry me."

"But how are we going to get you back to the parking lot?" Claire asked.

"Carefully," he replied with a grin. "Very carefully. I'm old, but as long as someone's always supporting me, I'll be fine."

* * *

It took quite some time, and there were plenty of iffy and scary moments, but twenty-five minutes later, they were back at the parking lot safely.

"Over there, guys," Bradley said, pointing to the far end of the parking lot. "Gimme a hand."

Bradley's car was hidden behind a bunch of bushes. The bushes looked so natural that they didn't notice until getting closer that his car was actually even there. The weather gods had uprooted and dropped bushes on and around his car.

"We don't have to move them all," Bradley instructed. "Just enough of them to get my car out."

It didn't take very long to move the ones in front of his car, plus the few blocking the driver's door.

Bradley started the car, revved the engine loudly a few times, and then pulled the car out of its hiding spot. Peter and Neil then pulled branches off the roof and hood.

"Okay, Nik and Claire," Bradley said. "Looks like you two beautiful young ladies are with me."

* * *

"I'll explain the route as we go," Peter said to Neil from the backseat, where he and Mr. Winchester were sitting in order to make a private conversation possible. "Unless you remember?"

"Nah, I don't," Neil replied. "I mean, I was only there that one time, which was, like, four months ago. And I wasn't driving, so I wasn't really paying much attention."

Peter gave Neil the first half of the instructions, which were pretty straight-forward.

"Neil, please put these on," Mr. Winchester said, passing Neil a pair of heavy-duty safety headphones.

"You're joking, right?" Neil said. "You don't trust me?"

"I completely trust you, Neil," he replied. "But for all our safety, it's best that you not hear this now. It might make you too uncomfortable to drive."

"Alright," Neil replied, getting ready to put the headphones on. "But hold on a sec. Where did you get these from?"

"I carry them everywhere I go," Mr. Winchester replied. "Doctor's orders. I have bad tinnitus, and loud noises quickly make it worse."

"Ah," Neil said, nodding while he adjusted them to fit snugly. He gave them the thumbs up, which meant they could begin their conversation.

"Okay, Peter," Mr. Winchester said softly "What I'm about to tell you is, well, of utmost importance."

"I gathered that," Peter replied quickly and inquisitively.

"It's about the reason why I know we'll be seeing them again," Mr. Winchester whispered. "I have something they want."

Peter knew Mr. Winchester would continue, so he remained silent.

"But first I need to quickly explain," said Mr. Winchester, "about Zoltan and Xavier's great-grandfather. He was, at one time, the most powerful weather god ever. He also served as a lead weather god for sixty years. But he wasn't powerful due to luck, or due to diligent training. He was powerful because he possessed an amulet. This one-of-a-kind amulet, when worn, increases a weather god's powers at least 100-fold, or possibly even a thousand. No one knows how he came to own the amulet in the first place. And his family has always kept its existence a secret."

"Hold on a sec," Peter said, interrupting Mr. Winchester. He leaned forward, took the headphones off Neil's ears and said, "Turn left at the next intersection, and then right just before the cornfield."

"Roger," Neil replied.

Peter then let go of the headphones, in order to block Neil's ears from hearing the rest of the conversation.

"Ouch!" Neil yelped.

"Sorry," Peter apologized. "Guess I released those a little too quickly."

"But when people got too suspicious about why he was so unbelievably powerful," Mr. Winchester continued, "he decided it was time to hide the amulet. He should've thrown the stupid thing off into outer space, but he just couldn't. He wanted it to be accessible, just in case a planet was in peril, and then the amulet could be used to help save billions of lives."

"Don't tell me he gave the amulet to *you!?*" Peter asked.

"Gosh, no," Mr. Winchester replied. "He hid it in a place back on Sevlar, and—"

"Is that the shed!?" Neil said very loudly, something people often did when wearing headphones, as they couldn't accurately assess how loud their voices were.

Peter gave Neil the thumbs up, which Neil caught by looking in the rear-view mirror. He parked beside the shed, took off the headphones, and all three of them got out of the car.

It didn't require the presence of a professional C.S.I. to realize that the shed had been broken into. The door, which should have been locked, was wide open.

"Oh my," Mr. Winchester said as he quickly entered the shed.

Bradley's car had just arrived and parked, and they were opening the doors to get out.

"What's going on?" Bradley asked.

"The shed door was open," Peter said to Bradley. "Someone must have busted in. Wait here guys, I'll go in and check on Mr. Winchester."

The inside of the shed looked like it had been turned upside down. Everything that was always neatly lined up on the shelves was in a massive heap on the floor. Mr. Winchester was now on his hands and knees frantically pulling things out of the mess.

"This doesn't make sense," Peter said to him. "I mean, the only people who know how to get to this shed are you, me, and Nik, right? Well, I suppose Claire, Brad, and Neil were all here that one time, too. But no one out of our circle even knows this place exists. Plus, the lock on the door is not one that could be picked or broken easily."

"Maximilian, Aurora, and Cynthia have definitely been here," Mr. Winchester said.

Bradley's curiosity had gotten the better of him, and despite Peter's instructions to wait outside, he went in. "Whoa," Bradley said. "Looks like a hurricane came through here."

"Mr. Winchester thinks Maximilian, Aurora, and Cynthia broke in," Peter explained. "But that doesn't make any sense. How would they have known about the shed?"

"Umm..." Bradley said, looking very uncomfortable.

"Brad!?" Peter said strongly to him. "What happened? Did they threaten you or something? Did they force you to tell them about the shed and show them where it was?"

"Uh…" Bradley mumbled. "Well… not exactly."

Mr. Winchester sensed the hesitation in Bradley's voice, and quickly stood up and faced him. "Bradley," he said quite loudly. "If you have an explanation for this, then tell us. Now."

"Well, you see," he said, fumbling for the right words. "And you probably didn't know this, but Aurora and I kind of started, like, hanging out, and she—"

"Brad!" Peter said, cutting him off. "I don't care about you and your dating history."

"Okay, okay," Bradley replied, sweat forming on his brow. "When I was out with her once, she asked me if I knew anything about the puzzles and stuff you and Nik used for Zoltan."

"So you brought her here?" Peter yelled.

"Yeah," Bradley gulped. "But all we did was walk inside the shed, and then just look at the stuff in here for a while."

"But how did you get in?" Peter inquired angrily. "It was locked, and I have the only key."

"Petey," Bradley said in a somewhat sarcastic tone. "You've always hidden all your money, hockey cards, or anything else you don't want discovered in the same place: in the back corner of your sock drawer."

"So are you saying," Peter said angrily, "that you stole the key, drove her down here, and let her inside the shed?"

"This is not good," Mr. Winchester said, still digging through the pile. "Not good at all."

Feeling really uncomfortable, Bradley decided to leave the shed. He had screwed up. Plain and simple. And it was too late to undo it.

"What are you looking for?" Peter asked.

Mr. Winchester stood up and had a look of extreme concern on his face. "Peter," he said. "There is something extremely important I kept in here. It was a small box that said—"

Peter interrupted him. "That said *open after I pass away* on it, right?" he asked.

"Yes," Mr. Winchester replied. "That's the one. Inside that box, there was—"

"A map!" Peter said, interrupting him again.

"How do you know that?" Mr. Winchester asked. "I'm not dead yet. Did you already look inside it?"

Peter smiled. "Of course I did," he replied. "You know me. I can't leave any mysteries hanging."

"Well," the old man continued. "The map shows how to get to the entrance of where the amulet is hidden on Sevlar. And the clues written on the map are necessary to solve a series of puzzles and riddles between the entrance and the exact spot where the amulet itself is hidden. But now that they've got the map, it'll only be a matter of time before Xavier gets that amulet, and—"

"Nah," Peter said, cutting off Mr. Winchester for a third consecutive time. "They won't find the amulet. At least not with the map they've got."

"Sorry?" Mr. Winchester asked, very confused. "What do you mean?"

"When I took that box home and opened it for the first time," Peter explained, "it was clear that the map was something of great importance. Something that obviously shouldn't be kept in a shed in the middle of nowhere. So I took it out and—"

"Took it out?!" Mr. Winchester asked in shock. "Well then they'll come back here as soon as they see the box is empty."

Peter smiled again. "It's not empty," he said. "I drew a map that bore a smashing resemblance to the original one, and also wrote various hints and clues on the map."

"You mean," Mr. Winchester said, looking quite surprised. "You made a fake map? With fake clues? And put it back in the box? And then brought it back here?"

"Yup," Peter answered.

"Ingenious," Mr. Winchester said.

"But why were you given the map in the first place?" Peter questioned him.

"Their greatgrandfather decided to pass the map down to his eldest offspring," Mr. Winchester explained. "And he also instructed that the map always be given to the first-born son or daughter, from one generation to the next, but never until that person reached the age of eighteen. Xavier and Zoltan's father received it on his eighteenth birthday, in fact. But let's fast forward a little. Xavier ran off at fourteen, so his father was conflicted about what to do. He finally decided that he would give it to Zoltan, but considering Zoltan's behavior and attitude, he felt Zoltan wasn't ready for it at age eighteen. So instead, he asked me to hold on to the map, and instructed me to only tell Zoltan about it when he had matured enough."

"Okay, I see..." Peter said. "Anyway, Xavier and his cronies will be searching for years before they realize they have the wrong map."

Mr. Winchester's expression changed. "Years?" he said. "We could only wish. Your little map trick will fool them for a while, but not for long. At some point, Peter, they will come back to Earth. Back for us. And they'll use whatever means necessary to get the real map."

"So why don't I just burn it?" Peter suggested. "Then the amulet will be lost forever."

Mr. Winchester pondered Peter's idea.

"Everything okay in there!?" Nicola asked, standing a few paces away from the shed door.

"Yeah, we're fine!" Peter replied. "We'll be out soon!"

"Does Nicola, or anyone else, know about the map?" Mr. Winchester asked.

"Nope," Peter replied.

"Then let's keep it that way," the old man said.

"So do you want me to burn it?" Peter asked, referring back to his question again.

"Absolutely not," Mr. Winchester answered. "Like it or not, we are now involved in this. If you burn that map, Xavier's henchmen will burn your home, the whole town, and possibly the whole country out of revenge."

"Sounds like a catch-22 to me," Peter said.

"A what?" Mr. Winchester queried.

"Oops," Peter said, guessing Mr. Winchester wasn't familiar with that phrase.

"What I'm saying," Peter continued, "is that either way, we lose. If Xavier gets the amulet, he'll have his way with everyone and everything. He'll destroy whatever and whoever he pleases. If we burn the map, he'll kill us out of anger, so we still die."

"There is one other option, Peter," Mr. Winchester said. "Well, it's the only feasible one I can think of right now. And we'll have to do two things to make it succeed. First, we'll need to rescue Zoltan. And second, we'll need to get the amulet. If Zoltan has the amulet, he will be powerful enough to defeat Xavier."

"Hold on," Peter replied. "Both of those things are entirely impossible. We are on Earth and they are on Sevlar. Obviously, we can't get to Sevlar."

"We can get there," Mr. Winchester said with a wink. "But I'll save that explanation for another day. Your friends are already getting suspicious about what we are talking about. I need to plan this out more carefully before we make any moves."

Mr. Winchester and Peter were temporarily blinded by the sunshine as they walked out of the shed. "Nothing of importance missing," Mr. Winchester announced to Bradley, Nicola, and Claire.

"Whew!" Nicola replied. "We were getting worried."

She looked over at Peter—he was hiding something—as he had that "I'm not being one hundred percent honest" look on his face. Poor guy just couldn't lie at all... but she would find out the truth later.

CHAPTER 37

Peter woke up early on Christmas morning, long before the rest of his family would even consider getting out of bed. He went downstairs and looked at the array of presents surrounding their beautifully decorated "fake" Christmas tree.

He walked into the kitchen and turned on the coffee maker. His mom's nose was almost as good as a police dog's, so as soon as the scent drifted upstairs, she'd wake up, have a two-and-a-half-minute shower, and then order everyone to come downstairs for present opening.

Meanwhile, Peter poured himself a glass of pulp-free orange juice, turned up the thermostat, and sat down on the big living room sofa. He looked out the large window at the thick, fresh snow that had fallen last night.

Then he smiled. "Oh, Pete, sometimes you surprise even yourself, don't you?" he said. He was imagining how Neil, Claire, and Nicola would react when they opened up their "gifts" from him this morning.

* * *

Since Nicola was an only child, and her parents weren't even a fraction as strict as Peter's, she was free to wake up and open her presents whenever she wanted. But it was such a cold day, and she was so comfortable in her warm bed, that it wasn't until her mom knocked on her bedroom door at 9:45 that she finally decided to get up.

For some odd reason she wasn't hungry, so she decided to open up her presents before having breakfast. Most were things she wanted and/or needed, plus a few were envelopes containing cash. The present from Peter, which was the size of a shoebox, she saved for last.

"Mom, Dad," she said. "No offense, but do you mind if I open this one in my room? It's from Pete."

"Not at all, dear," her mom replied, even though she was unbelievably curious about what was inside.

Nicola went back up to her room, sat down on her bed, and ripped off the wrapping paper. It was a shoebox, but gauging from its lightness, she knew there were no shoes inside. She opened it up to find that what it contained was... well... not what one would normally consider a "present." There were three letters of the alphabet, cut from pieces of cardboard: an "A," an "I," and a "Y." Plus there was a small note, folded in fours. She smiled while unfolding it, and then read it silently.

Well, I couldn't leave you hanging forever, now could I? You three told me about your riddles from that challenge when we were split up. And I told you about mine. But I never told you the answer, did I? (But it sure was fun to hear all your ideas for the answer!!)

But now that it's Christmas and your guesses (and Neil's and Claire's) have all been so brutally wrong, I thought I'd tell you the solution.

Just in case you forgot the riddle, it was:

$A \rightarrow A = 2$
$I \rightarrow I = 4$
$Y \rightarrow Y = ?$

And don't forget that there were four A's, nine I's, and six Y's written on the walls.

(Nik, are you sure you really want to read this? If not, just close the note, and keep guessing!)

Well, if you are still reading, then that means that curiosity got the better of you! But not to worry, it happens even to the best of us!

The trick here is that the arrow does NOT represent a mathematical sign.

The number on the right side of the equals sign indicates: <u>the number of ways you can flip the letter so that it will still look exactly the same</u>!

Grab the cardboard letters and follow my instructions. That'll make it way clearer.

First, put the "A" down. Now lift it and flip it to the right. It still looks like an "A," right? Now put it back where it started. Next, flip it to the left. Still looks like an "A" again, right? Put it back where it started again. Now flip it upwards. Now it's upside-down! Put it back a final time. Flip it downwards. Upside-down "A" again!" So the number of ways the "A" can be flipped in order to keep it as an "A" is two.

Now try the "I." Tell me how many of the four flips makes it stay the same? All four, right?

Now grab the "Y" and try it... Just like the "A" – it only looks the same when flipped left or right, so two ways! So there you go! The answer was door 2!

Merry Christmas, Nik!!

She shook her head in disbelief. Only the girlfriend of Peter would be happy to receive a present like this...

Thank you for reading *Extremely Puzzled*. I hope you liked the story, the new characters, and (most importantly) the puzzles! If you enjoyed this book, I would be thrilled beyond words if you took a minute to review it on Amazon or goodreads. Thank you so much!

If you have any questions or comments, please e-mail me anytime (pj@pjnichols.com) – there is nothing that brings a bigger smile to my face than hearing from a reader! Remember to check out the puzzles on my website (pjnichols.com) – there are some cool, head-scratching ones that will surely put your problem-solving skills to the test!

Sincerely,
P.J. Nichols

Acknowledgements

My awesome family and amazing friends, who give me so much energy and happiness that I feel like... breakdancing! (Don't worry, Freddy! I won't actually do it. Not that it wouldn't be fun to try, but my coordination is so poor that I would likely end up with at least one of my limbs in a cast...)

And speaking of family, I want to say an extra *Thank You* to my son, (age 10 at the time I wrote this book) who came up with one of the puzzles in Book 3. Can you guess which one? (If you'd like to know, e-mail me at pj@pjnichols.com and I'd be happy to let you know!)

Thomas, the creative and talented artist who spends countless hours designing the fantastic covers you see on all the Puzzled books.

Dalan, who narrates all the audiobooks to a quality above and beyond what I ever thought was possible.

Each and every reader, who I truly hope enjoyed reading the first three books as much as I enjoyed writing them!

About the Author

P.J. Nichols, for his entire life, (well, not including when he was a baby...) has always been fascinated by how much fun it is to "get your brain moving." Can you imagine a 10-year-old attempting a 1000-piece puzzle without looking at the box? Or thinking up and doing science experiments in the kitchen? Or making an obstacle course in a nearby park out of things he picked out randomly from the garage?

Well... P.J. hasn't changed one bit since then, as he still does the exact same things now!

P.J. considers himself incredibly lucky. He loves his day job (teaching), his weekend and evening job (writing the Puzzled books!), and all the joys of being a husband and father.

He still has many innovative, original, and intriguing riddles and puzzles in his mind. And he can't wait to put those into the next book of the Puzzled series!

To find out more about P.J.
(and try some cool puzzles!) visit
pjnichols.com

Printed in Great Britain
by Amazon

16804361R00141